The Rider and His Horse

The Rider and His Horse

ERIK CHRISTIAN HAUGAARD

Illustrated by Leo and Diane Dillon

1968

HOUGHTON MIFFLIN COMPANY BOSTON

Other Books by

ERIK CHRISTIAN HAUGAARD

Hakon of Rogen's Saga

A Slave's Tale

Orphans of the Wind

The Little Fishes

LIBRARY OF CONGRESS CATALOG CARD NUMBER: 68-29900

PRINTED IN THE U. S. A.

CONTENTS

For the
Chaverim of *Kibbutz Shomrat*
for their kindness
to the stranger
within their gates.

I will sing unto the Lord, for he hath triumphed gloriously: the horse and his rider hath he thrown into the sea.

Exodus, 15.

PREFACE

THE MAN without a past is a fiction; even willful ignorance cannot erase our history. Only in eternal night will man be shadowless, and the past not follow the present into the future. Because the past is part of us, we must learn from it. Knowledge of the past — of history — gives perspective to our world. Without that knowledge our loneliness would be harder to bear and sorrow would easily crush us.

Our technical advances have blinded us. Between us and reality stands a flat screen, a box of tubes and wires that proclaims itself to be life. But still we bleed and still we cry and still we laugh and still we long for something that is beyond us: something we cannot quite grasp. We are men longing to be Gods. We are eternal caterpillars doomed never to be butterflies, only to know of them.

In THE RIDER AND HIS HORSE I have written of an era in history when a nation died, only to rise — as the bird phoenix — from its ashes. The times of the Kings of Judea were over: the time of the warrior, the time of the sword. When the Greeks were defeated their Gods died, too. The Roman Gods could not even live as long as the empire they had created. But the Lord of the Jews was not only a warrior, he was a poet, as well. The sword fell from his hand but the Book remained, and it proved itself a fortress that two thousand years of siege could not conquer.

My story is the end of an era, a story of bloodshed and cruelty. But the story of the end must also be the story of the beginning. The Romans thought that by defeating Eleazar ben Ya'ir they had destroyed a nation, not knowing that a people, who through the next two thousand years would weave their culture through half the population of the world, had survived.

THOSE WHO NEVER LOSE | 1

"THE ZEALOTS are standing now on their mountain, looking down upon the Sea of Asphalt; and they cannot conceive that their fortress can fall. They are less than a thousand men, but since they have food and water for thirty thousand, they think themselves unconquerable. Eleazar ben Ya'ir looks out over the empty, lifeless desert and thinks himself a prophet; at night he sleeps in King Herod's palace and dreams he is King of Judea. But the Masada is conquered before it has even been besieged, for without Jerusalem and the rest of Judea, it is but a stone in the desert." Joseph ben Matthias looked out through the open door towards the garden, where a scarlet red bush bloomed. "Only a madman expects to harvest in the season when the grain is only sprouting or to get milk from a barren cow."

Again the speaker paused and it occurred to me that the pauses were as carefully timed by Joseph ben Matthias as his words were chosen. I glanced at my father; he was gazing with admiration at his friend. My father appeared fatter when he was sitting than when he stood. The sunlight shone on his balding head and made it shine like polished wood. 'He is a wine merchant,' I thought, 'and he looks like one; but he would like to have been a scholar. He is a fool!' I turned my head away, for how can one look at one's father whom one loves, after acknowledging that he is a fool.

"David, here," my father nodded towards me, "would fight the whole war over again." His smile hurt me, for in it I could read two things: that he did not understand me and that he was proud of me.

"Ah, the young! They are always ready for war! Always looking for a Goliath to kill." Joseph ben Matthias looked at me approvingly, but I suspected that his smile was a compliment to my father's wealth rather than to me personally.

Besides, he had misjudged me, for I had no longing for war, nor did I think that young men made wars: old man make them and young men die in them. But I did not want to be drawn into a discussion, so I said,

"I did not choose the name David. It was given to me. I might have been called Saul or Jonathan."

My father laughed. "No, you couldn't have. You are called after my brother, who died a year before you were born."

"Of course," I muttered. Speaking a little louder and glancing at Joseph ben Matthias, I added, "My uncle was a wine merchant, as my father is. He could neither sing nor play the harp."

Joseph ben Matthias frowned and again his gaze fell upon the scarlet bush in the garden.

'Now he hates me,' I thought, 'for such a man doesn't want youth to think. He wants them to be as dogs, to lick his fingers and look up at him with trusting eyes. If young men have opinions, it irritates their elders, makes them think that they have failed. This is the way God must have felt when he discovered that Adam and Eve had eaten of the fruit of the Tree of Knowledge.' My thoughts pleased me and I imagined my father with a sword of flames throwing me out of his house.

"And what will happen now? . . . Now that the war is lost?"

Joseph ben Matthias did not answer my father's question at once. He brought his hands together in front of himself and let each finger meet its brother; then he contemplated them. His fingers were long and slender: a scholar's hands. "The war was lost because when there are two Jews, you have two opinions. If you have two Jewish soldiers, you have two commanders. We have only one God, but we have as many interpretations of his words as we have people. In the courtyard of the Temple the lowest sandal maker, with a torn prayer shawl, thought himself a better interpreter of the Torah than the high priest. And that is why the Temple was destroyed. The Romans have more gods than they can count but they will follow their emperor to Hades without noticing the road they are traveling." Joseph ben Matthias snorted with anger.

'It is true what they say of him,' I thought. 'Joseph ben Matthias will go to Rome and serve the emperor, but only because the emperor is not a Jew. If he had been a Jew, Joseph ben Matthias would have acted as the sandal maker' . . . And I hated myself for having wanted to visit Joseph ben Matthias and even for having begged permission of my father to accompany him on this trip. I should have stayed at home in Tyre and listened to the news of the Jews' defeat around the supper table. Dreams are for the night, when eyes are closed: not for the day, for the open eye. Suddenly I felt ashamed, as if by being here I, too, were responsible for the defeat of Our People. I looked at the face of Joseph ben Matthias, who once had commanded the Judean forces in the Galilee, and I thought, 'That man is made of pride and vanity, and that is why he wants to be a Roman — and yet, for the same reason, he will not give up being a Jew.' Then I promised myself not to speak with him again.

"How true . . . How true." My father was agreeing with Joseph ben Matthias. "Only the other day a poor farmer with a small vineyard told me . . ." My father stopped talking. A group of Roman soldiers were walking along the street on the other side of the garden wall. They were talking in loud voices; I think they were drunk. My father's face darkened with displeasure; then, because I found that I, too, was frowning I grinned.

"I shall write the history of this war, the true history of . . . of . . ." Joseph ben Matthias hesitated and then said forcefully, "Of the Jewish War."

"It is not over yet!" I exclaimed. So quickly had I forgotten my promise to myself. But only a Roman would have said "The Jewish War"; a Jew would have called it "The Roman War."

"The Masada. You are still thinking of the Masada, which will fall before we celebrate the next Passover, maybe earlier."

I looked into the face of Joseph ben Matthias and said, "Like Jotapata?"

"No!" ben Matthias shouted at me. "Not like Jotapata! The commander of that city saw that the city was lost and then, like an honorable man, thinking of the lives of the people and putting their welfare higher than his personal wish for glory, he surrendered . . . Herod's Masada is now a haven for wolves and wolves do not surrender, they are killed!"

"He is but a child," my father apologized hastily.

Joseph ben Matthias had turned his back towards both of us and I looked anxiously at my father. He was confused and unhappy; for his sake I begged ben Matthias' pardon. "Forgive me, Joseph ben Matthias. Forgive me. I cannot hide behind my father's excuses. I am fourteen and have been bar mitzvahed."

"*I will sing unto Jehovah, for he is mighty and exalted: The horse and his rider hath he thrown into the sea.*" Although Joseph ben Matthias' voice was low, every word could be heard as clearly as if he had shouted. "We are the horse and his rider and God has left us. He has thrown the sons of Israel into the sea." He turned to face me.

'He speaks like a prophet,' I thought, 'but has not a prophet's face. He knows of God, but he does not speak with Him.'

"Whatever we do, all is vanity. The Masada was Herod's dream and Herod was a king and dreamed a king's dream. We are not the seed from which the crop of God's righteousness should spring. We are the chaff and the chaff blows where the wind commands."

My father had not understood the meaning of his friend's words, but he loved to listen to the speech of priests and wise men. It pleased him as music did. In our home in Tyre, he invited to his table any priest or holy man who passed through the city.

"Moses was speaking of our enemies not of us: The

horse and his rider were the soldiers of the Pharaoh, who were following the Children of Israel as they crossed the Red Sea." My father glanced at me timidly. He wished I had not spoken. I was his only son, and he hoped that one day I would become a scholar, a wise man; and that dream was dear to him.

"How do we know the will of God? We do not study the entrails of birds as the Romans do, to find out the wishes of their gods. But it is equally foolish not to study history and learn from it. God has made a Covenant with us; and now, because of our failings, He has abandoned us. We became like other nations and thought in their terms; for this He will punish us and we shall never be a nation again. We became the rider and his horse, and God will always throw them into the sea . . ." He took a step towards me. "You are a foolish boy. How do you know what the Commander of Jotapata saw when he stood on the walls of the city? Do you think the Roman shields blinded him? Do you think he used them as a mirror for his fear? Or was each shield a letter? The vast army that surrounded him a book?"

Now I looked away. As I tried to imagine Joseph ben Matthias standing on the ramparts of Jotapata gazing at the Roman legions who had laid siege to the city, I realized that I did not know what he — Joseph ben Matthias, Commander of Jotapata — had thought. How did I know the reasons for his giving up the city? I did not believe — though I had been told it often — that Joseph ben Matthias had surrendered for money. I wished I were not in the room, but outside in the bright sunlight of Caesarea.

THOSE WHO ALWAYS LOSE | 2

CAESAREA is Herod's city. No, the whole country is his! The murderer of his own children, that braggart, he will live! Why did he want all these monuments to himself? He was a man, he would die, for all men must die. Was that the reason, his knowledge of death?

"Alms, alms for the unfortunate." The beggar was sitting on the pavement, his withered leg carefully displayed.

I did not want to look at him. I have never liked to look at beggars. They remind me of my own good fortune. Silently, they ask me: If you had been born with a withered leg, would you not be sitting here? It is different with those beggars who are the cause of their own misfortune — even those who are the victims of war. I can say to myself: He was a fool, serves him right; this would never happen to me! But those who are maimed from birth remind me that life is a lottery, that there is no justice. The dice roll across the table and eyes proclaim the winner.

I dropped a small coin into the cupped hand of the beggar. He did not even look at it, nor did he thank me. 'He knows his role well,' I thought. 'He knows that he is not a man, but a message from God, saying that all is vanity.' I had been told that Herod hated beggars and that he would not allow them in Caesarea.

I had escaped from the house of Joseph ben Matthias and now I was on my way to the harbor. I love the sea. Even when I was very young, I would try to escape from the watchful eye of the bondswoman to run to the harbor. Although my mother was not very strict, she would beat me for this, for she feared the sea. To her it was evil; she said that it belonged to the Romans and that their gods ruled it.

The harbor was crowded with ships. Most of them were Roman: ships that had transported troops from Egypt to Titus, to fill the ranks of his army that was conquering Judea. Now they were being loaded with slaves: Jews who had been captured when Jerusalem fell and were now to be sent to Greece.

"Do you want to see the slaves?"

A soldier had called to me; and though I could see the three rows of human beings lined up on the pier very well from where I stood, I followed him.

"The emperor is going to build a canal near Corinth. They are going to dig it."

I had heard of the canal. My father had spoken of it enthusiastically; it would save many days' sailing from Tyre to Brindisi.

"We are using the whole fleet to transport them. Already ten thousand have been sent." The number impressed the soldier so much, that he repeated it, "Ten thousand!"

I looked up at him. He did not hold a high rank. His clothing was poor and he spoke Latin badly. "Where are you from?" I asked.

He turned away and said arrogantly, "I am a Roman citizen."

I guessed him to be Greek, and therefore spoke to him in that language. "Many a Roman citizen was born far from Rome."

"I come from the south of Greece, near where they say King Nestor's palace stood."

"I have heard," I said, "that there is a treasure buried there. A seaman who came from that place told me about it. It is called Pylos."

"When my father was a young man, he found a gold coin; and he spent the rest of his life looking for the treasure, but he found nothing more."

"It is easier to make a treasure than to find one."

These words were not my own, I had heard my father say them.

"I know it is there!" The soldier spoke passionately. "They have all searched in the wrong places; the palace was not by the sea." The soldier gestured towards the slaves. "If I had only a hundred men to dig, I should find it."

I had been staring at the slaves. One of them caught my glance with his own, and I turned away.

"Were you at Jerusalem?" I asked the soldier.

"I was everywhere . . . The whole war through." He seemed angry as if the question had offended him.

"At Jotapata, too?"

"Yes, but that was easy. No, Jerusalem was different. They fought like wolves." The soldier flung out his arm threateningly at the slaves. "They will dig the canal now. They will dig until they die and they will never see Jerusalem again."

I doubt that any of the slaves who stood near enough to hear us understood Greek, but they could guess that the soldier was talking about them. The slave who had caused me earlier to turn my face away now called out to me in Hebrew, "Who are you, stranger, that you need look at us now that we are no more than beasts?"

"I am from Tyre," I answered. "And because a man shares the lot of a beast, he does not become one."

"Give me the gold ring on your finger."

My left hand touched the ring on the middle finger

of my right hand; but I did not take it off. "The soldiers would take it away from you."

"I shall hide it."

I glanced at the Roman. He was trying to understand what was being said, but he knew no Hebrew. While the slave looked at me pleadingly and yet with indignation, as if he were accusing me of some unforgivable sin, I said to the soldier in Greek, "I know that man." I pointed to the slave. "He is strong but has a weak head. He used to be a bondsman of my father; but my father sent him away because he did not keep the Sabbath." Why had I added to my lie the story of the broken Commandment? Was it because I had already decided to give him the ring?

"Then he shan't mind Greece, for there there will be no Sabbath."

We were so near the slaves that we could smell their unwashed bodies; and while I spoke loudly in Greek for the benefit of the soldier, I let the ring pass from my hand into that of the slave. "I shall tell my father that I have seen this man, who served him so badly — he, who is such a good master ought to know that fate has punished a disobedient fellow like this one."

As I took a step closer to the Roman, the slave said in Hebrew, just loud enough for me to hear him, "The blessing of the Lord be on you!"

Now I wanted to go away. I debated with myself how much, or rather how little, I should give the soldier. "They smell . . . I have seen enough of them,"

I said, turning my back on the slaves. To my surprise I could see in the face of the Greek, who called himself a Roman, that he was disgusted by my display of indifference. This caused me to drop back into my purse the tiny coin that I had been about to give him and select a larger one; although the first was as much as he had a right to expect from a youth, though my clothes spoke of wealth.

"May the winds blow against your back and the gods protect you!" he said gratefully.

"May you return to your home and find your treasure," I said, and walked swiftly from him.

The soldier caught up with me. "I am called Virtus of Pylos. I am stationed at the Roman camp just beyond the city. If your father should be interested in the treasure, he can find me. Tell your father that you know a man who knows, for certain, where King Nestor's treasure is buried, the treasure that King Nestor brought home from Troy." Now he lowered his voice and looked about him. "Tell him if he will pay for the slaves to dig, we can share equally. Equally, my boy."

I smiled for I knew that my father was not interested in buried treasures. The soldier misunderstood my grin; he thought he had been too familiar and said apologetically, "Tell your father that I shall serve him well and that he will be pleased with me."

"I shall tell him what you have said." For the last time, I looked at the man. He belonged to no guard regiment. He had fought a war, and yet he was as poor as the day he had landed in Judea. Soon he would be moved to another place where there was a revolt, another campaign to fight in another foreign country. If he did not die in battle, he would end begging in the streets. He was not a Roman citizen, of this I was certain. He belonged to some auxiliary regiment and no guards would drink a bowl of wine with him.

When I returned to the town I felt restless. I went to the inn where my father and I were staying. There I washed myself and changed my clothes; then I laid down on the couch. My father still had not come back from the house of Joseph ben Matthias. I wondered what I should say to my mother when she discovered that I no longer had the ring which she had given me. It had belonged to her father, who had died before I was born. From the ring my thoughts wandered to the slave: What would he do with it? Where could he hide it? A slave may not own property and any soldier who saw it could take it away from him.

I fell asleep and dreamed that I was a slave. I was dirty and I did not care. In the middle of the dream I became a Roman, a soldier. I wore a gold band around my arm; I must have been a general.

I woke. It was dusk. I lay listening to the noises from the street. 'What are you?' I asked myself. 'I am nothing. The son of a rich merchant from Tyre, whose father wants him to become a scholar, a student of the Torah. I am still only part of my father's dreams.' But I had dreamed that I was a Roman general. I turned towards the wall. "I wish I had not spoken to the soldier," I said out loud. I closed my eyes and tried to sleep again.

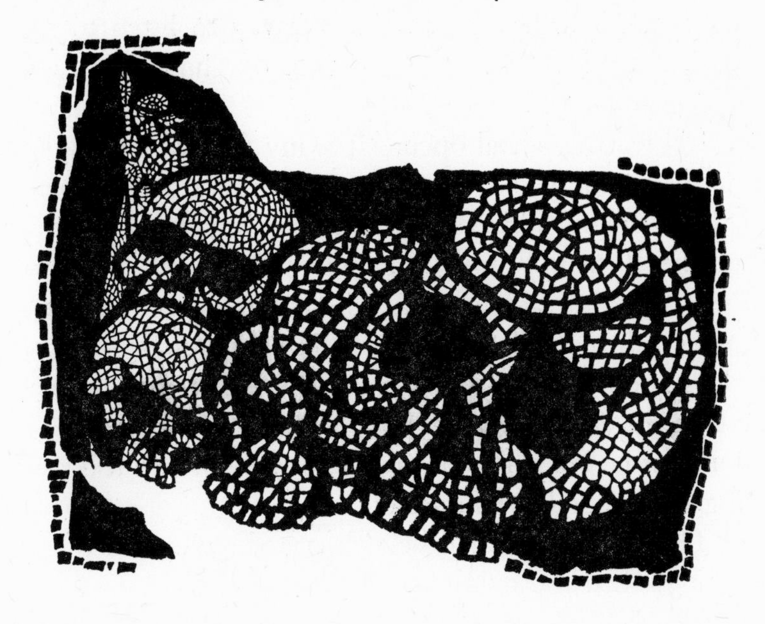

I MUST HAVE fallen asleep again, for when I woke the sun had set and the room was dark. "Father," I called into the darkness.

No one answered. I rose from the couch and fumbled my way to the door. I could hear voices from the downstairs rooms; it could not be late. For a while I remained in the doorway. Halfway down the stairs an oil lamp burned in a niche; but the wick had not been properly trimmed and it was smoking. It pleased me to stand there. For a moment I became a child again; a child who had been put to sleep but because of loneliness had sneaked to the stairway to listen to the voices from below. Like the inn, our house in Tyre had two floors.

I heard the portal open. 'It is my father,' I thought, 'he has come back. He is happy because he has spent all afternoon talking about the Torah and the politics of the Roman Empire. He will tell me what Joseph ben Matthias said; but he will not tell me about the purse full of gold coins that he has given to him. And the reason that he will not tell me is not that he suspects the friendship of Joseph ben Matthias, as I do, but that he is a generous man who would think it boasting to tell of his kindnesses.'

The door to the hall below opened and a gust of air extinguished the oil lamp. "Father!" I called.

Our servant, Saul, answered me, "I am coming, David. Your father sent me to tell you to come to Joseph ben Matthias' house. You shall have your supper there."

I did not want to go and I considered sending Saul back with some excuse. A tiny light appeared in the darkness; it was one of the servants of the inn. Having noticed that the lamp on the stairs was not burning, he lighted it.

"You will have to trim the wick," I said, but he continued on his way, as if he had not heard me.

"Two men have come from Jerusalem. Your father wants to hear their news," Saul explained as he slowly climbed the stairs.

"Who are they?"

"One is the cousin of a high priest. The other is a teacher."

"And what news do they bring? What news that we do not know already?"

"I don't know. They travel poorly; they have no servants." Saul had come with my father from Nazareth, when they both had been young men. He had been my father's bondsman, but had stayed with my father as a servant after his seven years of bondage were passed. Saul gloried more in my father's wealth than any member of the family.

"All right, I shall come," I said.

" 'God has been on our side; it is God who brought down the Jews from their strongholds, for what could human hands or instruments do against such towers?' " The man was not speaking, he was declaiming.

No one in the room had noticed my entrance.

"These were the words of Titus when he entered Jerusalem and saw our walls and our towers."

'That is the teacher,' I thought, 'not the cousin of the high priest.' The speaker was a small man with dark brown hair that rested on his shoulders. Now I noticed the man sitting in the shadows near the far wall; he was thinner and probably taller than the speaker. He, I assumed, must be the cousin of the high priest.

"I would like to write down what Titus said. Please, repeat the words slowly." Joseph ben Matthias was standing before a desk, on which were parchment and writing materials.

As I heard them repeated, I wondered, 'Has Titus ever spoken these words?' These were not the sentiments of a brute like Titus; they were hearsay that the teacher had phrased carefully for some purpose of his own.

My father finally saw me and called me to his side. He introduced me to the other guests, but none of them paid any attention to me. I suppose they thought me a child.

"All the walls have been torn down. There is no Temple any more!" The teacher's voice sounded triumphant as if he were telling of a victory not a defeat. "Was not the Temple, itself, an image? Was it not the calf, the golden calf?" The teacher was perspiring, his forehead was damp.

I sat close enough to the cousin of the high priest to see that he was smiling. Joseph ben Matthias looked troubled. I knew that he was a Pharisee, as were my father and most of the Jews; but he also prided himself on having many high priests in his family, so by birth he was a Sadducee.

"God said that he would speak through the sons of Aaron," Joseph ben Matthias began scornfully. "He knew the minds of His people well, when He made this stipulation. If all the Jews can be teachers and interpreters of the Torah, who will sow the grain and make our sandals?"

The cousin of the high priest laughed with delight. But the teacher was so carried away by his own thoughts that he did not realize that he was being made a fool of, and went on excitedly.

"The Torah, the Ark, must be our new Temple; and every man must study. We shall make new offerings, in prayer and in reading; so God can see that we can read our misfortune and learn from it; and from his words shall we learn to correct our faults. We have been vain; now we must seek humility. We have been stiff-necked, now we must learn to be meek."

Only my father gave his full attention to the teacher. Only my father did not realize that this was a speech that the teacher had given many times.

"Jerusalem has fallen, so that God's words can live!"

The teacher's voice seemed to resound. When I was eight years old, I had been in Jerusalem and seen the Temple. Although I had heard of its magnificence over and over again, it had impressed me beyond my dreams; and now the teacher's crowing so enraged me that tears came into my eyes.

"Oh, Jerusalem!" he continued. "You were destroyed so that you may never fall again! Jerusalem, you are nothing but rubble now; but if I whisper your name, my eyes fill with tears. They took the city from your name, so that your name could become the city! . . . Caesarea, Rome, Alexandria, you stand with your temples, your pillars of marble; but your names are only words!"

"Tomorrow, we shall return to Tyre." My father was speaking. Bowls of fruit had been placed on the low table from which we had eaten.

"Do you think they will have use for a teacher there?" The teacher, whose name I now knew was Ephraim, looked beseechingly at my father. My father appeared uncomfortable and tried to seem absorbed in thought. "I want to serve Our Lord and live like a humble man."

"If you study the Torah as diligently as you ate of my meal, you will be famous for your learning."

The teacher blushed and pulled back his hand that had been about to reach for a piece of fruit. "In Jerusalem there have been bad times," he said with embarrassment.

"You can travel with us to Tyre tomorrow, if you wish," my father said. The teacher smiled happily and I wondered if he realized that it was Joseph ben Matthias' insult that had gained him my father's pity.

"I have two wives and two children."

My father shrugged his shoulders, indicating by this movement that the teacher was welcome to bring his family.

"Over a hundred thousand died of starvation in Jerusalem. The stink of the dead and decomposing bodies made many Romans vomit; so the corpses of the murdered and the starved made the stomachs of the conquerors rebel, that is our victory." This was the first time I had heard the cousin of the high priest speak.

His voice was thin like a woman's. "My father and mother were killed and I could not bury them. All this, so Ephraim, here, can teach the Torah." To our horror, he laughed loudly.

'You can see too much,' I thought, 'then you are blind.'

No one could speak now. After a long silence, my father mumbled that we would have to leave Caesarea early in the morning. Joseph ben Matthias did not try to persuade us to stay. The teacher followed us, but the cousin of the high priest remained.

AT THE CROSSROADS | 4

WE LEFT CAESAREA early in the morning, traveling in the company of two other merchants and their bondsmen and slaves. Ten soldiers from the garrison at Caesarea, who had been hired to protect us, were also part of the caravan. We wanted to be in Tyre by the eve of the Sabbath and had only three days for our journey. Most of us were on foot, so we had little time to waste. I wore a little dagger at my side and as I walked I tried to think what I would do if we were attacked by brigands. It was not an idle daydream; in Judea, in Samaria, and the Galilee many caravans had been attacked. As a child I had often imagined myself in this dangerous position. Then I had seen myself as either the hero who saved the caravan or as a captive of the bandits, whom they made into their slave. But now as we slowly made our way along the barren road north, away from Caesarea, I found that reality did not lend itself to such dreams. 'If we are attacked,' I thought, 'we shall all be killed.' I was convinced that our guards would be the first to flee; if, indeed, they did not join our attackers. They were the most stupid and brutal looking men I had ever seen.

The teacher had joined us with his wives and children. The youngest child was a baby, which one of his wives carried in her arms. She was a strong woman and taller than her husband; nevertheless, she appeared to fear him.

'He grovels before other men,' I thought, 'but at home he is a despot.'

His other wife was a much older woman. His older child was a girl. Her name was Miriam. She was younger than I, but her back was already bent from working, as a slave's is.

"Do you think you will like Tyre?" I asked as I approached her. She was carrying a bundle which I had thought contained clothing, but now, on closer examination, I realized was filled with kitchen utensils. She did not reply to my question. "Your sack is heavy," I said. "One of the donkeys can carry it."

The girl shook her head but I called Saul; and we strapped her bundle to one of the donkeys.

"I think you will like Tyre. There is a harbor and a great many ships come there."

The girl finally turned to look at me; but her expression was strange, as if I had been talking in a foreign language. "Tyre is different from Jerusalem . . . I have been in Jerusalem once." Still she said nothing. She walked with her head stooped forward, as if she were fascinated by the movements of her feet in the sand.

"Answer the young man, Miriam!" Unnoticed, the teacher had come up behind us.

"Yes, father," the girl said hurriedly. Her voice had more strength than I had expected.

Under his arm the teacher carried one of those woven bags which you see in pairs draped over donkeys. Miriam offered to take it from him; but he refused to let her, smiling at me as he said no.

'He is a flea,' I thought. 'He will hang on my father.' I felt angry and my thoughts came in a rush. 'He is like a merchant who deals in other people's kindness: he can appreciate the good heart only in so far that he can profit from it.'

"Your father is a very wise man," the teacher was saying.

While I mumbled my thanks, I thought, 'No, wise he is not or he would never have invited you to his table.'

"The merchant and the scholar in one: that is the great future for our people."

"I think that if we had had better soldiers than merchants, and better generals than scholars, we might have been a free people yet." I had not looked at the teacher as I spoke but at Miriam, whose lips parted slightly.

"The sword is for the brute. We are God's people!"

I despised this argument; I had heard it since I had been big enough to eat at table with my father. "Was not Saul a fighter? And David?"

"Saul transgressed the Commandments of the Lord, and God let him fall. David . . . Was not his great-grandmother Ruth the Moab, a woman not of our people?"

I laughed at the teacher. So this was his scholarship, to use the Torah to snicker at what was greater than himself! He, who had to beg favors of a wine merchant to obtain food, could censure dead kings. He was a gossip monger of the dead.

The teacher started to speak but I cut him short. "My name is David. My father named me not only after his dead brother but also after the king." I could see the anxiety in his eyes and I despised him. "My father told me the story of Ruth when I could sit on his knees."

"You must answer the young man, when he speaks to you, Miriam; lest he should think you are not well brought up," the teacher said severely. Miriam nodded but her head remained bent; and I wondered whether she understood that he was expressing towards her the irritation which he dared not direct towards me. Suddenly, as if he had thought of something very important which he must say to him, the teacher left us and rushed up to my father.

My father was riding a horse. This was a matter of pride, for he was a poor rider and would have preferred a donkey. My father was smiling gratefully. 'The teacher is praising me to my father,' I thought. I could not bear to see my father's delight; I flung back my head and looked up at the cloudless sky.

"Was it bad that she was a Moab? Ruth, I mean."

Hearing the girl speak was so unexpected that it took a moment to understand what she had said. "Ruth . . . Ruth lived a long time ago. If you came upon her grave, it would be dust."

Miriam frowned; she had not understood me; but then to her, maybe Ruth was not dead; for surely to her father, the teacher, she lived. "Ruth was a good woman," I explained. "She was courageous and kind. Is that not enough?" I pointed to a bush that was struggling to grow in the sand. "Look, is that like the bushes that grow near Jerusalem? Who knows the difference and who cares!"

Yet I, too, had cared once and not so long ago. I had studied the Torah each day and learned large sections by heart. That was until a year ago when my father had decided that I ought to know Greek better. This

his friend, Joseph ben Matthias, had suggested; and I was sent every day to a man who earned his living in Tyre by teaching his native language. My Greek teacher had called himself a philosopher and I had thought him wise. He had had contempt for the Torah and I had copied him; but when my year of study was nearing its close and I could both read and write in Greek, I also understood that my teacher only reflected the shadows of those greater than himself. One day on my way to his house, I passed through the market-place. There I saw a man with a monkey which he had brought from Africa. The monkey performed tricks for which the onlookers threw him coins. 'This monkey,' I thought, 'is like my Greek teacher.' I told my father that I did not wish to study Greek any more; but I did not return to my study of the Torah. I began to spend my time in the streets and in the harbor. I talked with sailors from distant lands, and I felt that all my reading had taught me nothing. 'Knowledge and wisdom are alive,' I thought. 'And all living things one must catch.'

"Did you see the slaves in the harbor of Caesarea?" I asked. Miriam nodded. "To be a slave . . . ," I said thoughtfully. "To be a slave, to have no will of your own. To obey and when the sun sets not even the night is your own, for you are too weary to dream. Some of the slaves were sons of Jerusalem; others were just poor people who had come to the city to celebrate Passover, the holiday that commemorates their forefathers' freedom from slavery. And now they, themselves, are slaves."

In the distance we could see the sea; Miriam turned her head towards it. "Only rich children are free," she said; but there was no bitterness in her voice. To her this was a truth so often proven that it did not even cause anger. "But they will take them away from their homes, from the place they know, and that is terrible."

"Do you think life is worse beyond that?" I pointed towards the horizon. There was no wind and the sea lay still and appeared like a blue desert.

Miriam raised her head. "Not for the people that live there; they have their homes, that is where they were born. Outside our little house in Jerusalem, there was an old fig tree . . ." The girl stopped talking. She was not used to expressing her thoughts in words, and finding the task difficult, she gave up.

'A tree,' I thought. 'Yes, a tree may be a home to a child as a vineyard is to a farmer. And those slaves, whom I saw in the harbor, they had a tree somewhere, a piece of land, or a house.' Did I have a tree? No, my father's vineyards were tended by his bondsmen and his slaves, and his house was cleaned by servants. Once there had been a dog; but my father did not like dogs and it was driven from our house by the servants with stones.

Ahead of us rose Mount Carmel. On the right were low hills covered with scrub trees. The earth was no longer sandy as it had been near Caesarea. A flock of sheep were grazing near the road. A short distance ahead of us the road divided. One continued along the coast towards Akko and this one we would follow. The other went inland to the ancient city of Megiddo, where it joined the road to Nazareth and the Sea of the Galilee.

The sun was high in the sky and now we were to rest and eat our midday meal. As we approached the crossroads, we saw the corpses of six men who had been crucified there. It had probably happened many days before; the lifeless bodies that hung from the crosses were rotting. I turned to Miriam; she was staring at the crosses. 'She must have seen worse,' I thought.

"When you came to Caesarea, didn't you see them?" she asked.

"We came by ship," I answered; then to make the sight less horrible, I said, "They were robbers."

"In Jerusalem, Titus stole the candlesticks from the Temple; and even from my father, poor as he is, the soldiers stole everything. They beat him and burned our house as punishment for hiding something that we did not have. If a priest from the Temple had not argued for us, we should have been sold as slaves, too."

"But these were robbers," I insisted. "Until a month ago, no traveler was safe on the road. They killed many people."

Miriam looked down at her feet and said no more. Beyond the crosses, a grove of trees cast shadows and we rested there. The servants unpacked the food. The soldiers sat in a group by themselves. They had brought their own food, but we were to supply them with wine. They did not try to conceal their contempt for us; and surely, they had more in common with the dead men on the crosses than they did with us.

The two merchants and my father ate together; the teacher sat near them, but my father did not ask him to join them. I sat by myself, but near Miriam and the teacher's wives. I saw they had no food and ordered Saul to give them some of ours. I noticed that although Saul, as always, obeyed me, he took no pleasure in fulfilling my wish.

CAPTURED! | 5

I HAD EATEN and was lying on my back looking up at the sky. A group of vultures were circling far above me. It was autumn but the sun was still hot, for it had not rained since the spring. The leaves of the trees were dark green and had no freshness in them. 'I am like those birds,' I thought. 'I belong nowhere. What am I? My name is David. I have read the Torah but I cannot believe that I am chosen by God. I am a grain of sand; the wind can lift and deposit me where it chooses. Jerusalem has fallen. They say that a hundred thousand people died there; and before they died they said prayers, that I, too, know. They mumbled words that I understand. They were my brothers, of my people; and yet, they were not. The heaviest burdens a man can bear are not stones, but thoughts of his own loneliness:

'My God, My God, why have you left me?
Why are you so far away that you cannot help me?
Why are my thoughts alone?'

I smiled, for the last words were not of the song; they were my own.

"Why are you smiling?" I turned. Miriam had sat down beside me. I wondered how long she had been there.

"Do you know David's Songs?" I asked.

"Yes and no," she replied. I waited but she did not explain.

"I had thought of one of the Songs. That is why I was smiling. I like them better than the Torah, don't you?"

She looked at the ground beside her, and I realized that she never looked up when she spoke. "I am a woman; of things like that, I may not have an opinion."

I grinned. "Are you a woman? I thought you were a girl."

My words had made her blush. She mumbled, "I am a child, but soon I shall be twelve and then I am a woman."

Feeling a little ashamed, I said more seriously, "If

you are still a child, you can think anything you like, for a child knows nothing, and therefore, cannot commit a sin."

"A child knows a lot," she said earnestly.

'Yes, she knows a lot,' I thought, 'but her knowledge has made her sad.'

"Strangers coming!" one of the soldiers called.

I jumped up but I could see no one. I looked in the direction from which we had come, then towards the road to Akko.

"Bandits!" someone screamed.

I grasped my dagger. "Where?" I shouted.

I heard the yelling of the brigands as they attacked. They were coming across the top of a low hill ahead of us. They were a ragged band; only their leaders were on horseback.

"Go to your father," I said to Miriam.

As they came towards us, most of the bandits were shouting but some were laughing; and I felt their laughter as an insult. 'I hate them,' I thought. 'Why weren't they all crucified?'

I felt an arm about my shoulder. It was my father. The two other merchants were standing behind him. 'He is not afraid,' I thought and I felt proud.

"We are too few, we cannot fight. We must try and bargain with them," said one of the merchants. He came from Sidon, a town north of Tyre.

My father smiled. "I am afraid that our bargaining

position is not very strong." He turned around and pointed behind us. Our escort were retreating as fast as their legs could carry them.

"Cowards!" I called after them.

My father shook his head. "They were part of an auxiliary regiment that had not been paid since they left Damascus. I did not expect them to be slaughtered for our sake; but I had hoped that the sight of them would be a shield and they might be useful against a single wolf; but against a whole pack . . ."

The robbers were surrounding us. Their leader was riding a white horse; over his shoulders was draped a scarlet cape. His men had stopped running; they knew they need not fear for their prey and they came towards us leisurely. Now the leader reined his horse before us. His cape was torn and dirty and his beard unkempt. He was laughing and I could see that two of his front teeth were missing.

"I am the King of Samaria!" he announced very slowly. Perhaps he thought we would miss the importance of his words if he said them quickly. I glanced at my father. He was smiling; yet there was no reason to smile for the Samaritans have no love for the Jews and much to revenge.

"We are peaceful travelers. What does the King of Samaria want from us?" My father bowed low, as if he were speaking to a real king.

For a moment the robber appeared confused, then he opened his mouth and laughed. "The King of Syria taxes you. Well, I am the King of Samaria and I will tax you, too."

"Syria has no king, only a Roman governor!" I said angrily. I turned to look at my father; he had closed his eyes and was shaking his head.

"We are poor merchants from Sidon and Tyre. We have but little gold and silver with us; but what we have, we shall be pleased to give the King of Samaria." My father walked up to the side of the leader's horse and held up his leather purse. It was snatched from my father's hand. The other two merchants stepped forward and offered their purses. The robber counted the coins in each and then shoved the purses into his girdle.

"It is not enough!" he said savagely.

'Now he is done being king,' I thought.

With a wave of his hand, the leader of the bandits directed the unloading of our donkeys; then our horses were led away. I glanced over my shoulder. In the far distance I could make out ten fleeing men. 'Soon they will be back at their garrison in Caesarea. They will tell what has happened to us, and — '

A woman cried out, and I saw one of the robbers carrying Miriam's bundle with the kitchen utensils in it away. The teacher was swaying back and forth, mumbling a prayer; his wives and children had hidden themselves behind him.

Now when all our property had been taken and there was nothing but the clothes that we were wearing for the robbers to steal, the "King of Samaria" galloped his horse in a circle around us. Suddenly he stopped and pointed at me, "Is that your son?"

"No!" my father shouted. "He is only a slave." Then, realizing that my clothes would belie his claim, he added, "I bought him from a rich Roman. He is to be the teacher of my son, who — Glory be to God! — is safe in my house in Tyre."

"Come here," the "king" beckoned.

As I walked towards the leader of the bandits I tried to catch his gaze.

"Did the old man speak the truth?"

Against my will, I turned to look at my father. His face was white; even a fool could read the truth in it.

"I will kill you both, if you lie."

"My father lied; but it is a lie that brings no shame to him, for a father must try to save his son."

The "king" grinned. "You also claim to come from Tyre. I think you come from Judea."

"See!" one of the robbers shouted, waving his arms. "He has a face like Eleazar the Murderer!"

My father said firmly, "It is true that my grandfather was born within the shadows of the wall of the Temple. It is also true that I keep the Law. I am a Pharisee who was born in Nazareth and came to Tyre when my face was yet beardless. As for Eleazar, are you talking of Eleazar ben Ya'ir who leads the defense of the Masada? I do not know him and I do not support his cause."

My father's cunning was wasted. In Samaria they knew of only one Eleazar, Eleazar ben Dinai. Perhaps, it had even been foolish of my father, for who had not heard of the raids of Eleazar ben Dinai and his followers against the Samaritans? Joseph ben Matthias called Eleazar ben Dinai a bandit, but others had called him the "Sword of Judea." Eleazar ben Dinai was dead. He had been crucified in Rome; but the hatred against him endured both among the Romans and the Samaritans.

"Kill them! Kill them!" several of the robbers screamed.

"In seven days, come back to this place and bring with you a hundred gold pieces, the kind the King of Syria uses." The leader of the bandits looked at me angrily. "Then you shall have your son back. If you come with soldiers then bring his burial garments."

My father's face was red with rage. I wanted to comfort him, so I said, "I am not afraid, father."

The "king" had heard me. He laughed as two of his men grabbed me. "I shall teach you to be afraid. I am as good a teacher as any Roman."

"I shall come alone here on the day that you have appointed," my father said, "and bring what you want."

My hands were being tied behind me; I could smell the robbers' breath.

"Shalom," the "king" laughed. "Peace be with you."

One of the robbers took me by the shoulders and turned me around; then he kicked me so I nearly fell. Not before we were in the hills did I have a chance to look back. My father was standing alone. The other merchants were talking to each other; they would tell the first Roman garrison they came to about the "King of Samaria." There was nothing my father could do to prevent them; and although it was too far away for me to make out his features, I imagined I saw the expression of hopelessness in his eyes.

"THE KING OF SAMARIA" | 6

ALL AFTERNOON we had marched. Now we were on the east side of Mount Carmel, north of the ancient city of Megiddo, where the Romans have a camp. In truth, we were not in Samaria, for Mount Carmel is beyond its borders; but I do not think the "king" took his title too seriously. Children play at being king. It is a magic word to all those whom age does not give wisdom. God gave the Children of Israel a king, after they had begged for one; and He had understood that they were not wise enough to understand Him and not strong enough not to want to imitate other nations.

At evening we camped and a guard was posted near me. He did not speak like a Samaritan and I spoke to him in the Syraic dialect, which I had learned in the streets of Tyre where it is spoken by some of the workmen and poorer tradesmen, many of whom do not speak Greek.

"Where do you come from?" I asked. I was sitting down but my hands were still tied behind my back and my wrists hurt.

"From Damascus, Judean dog!" he said and spat.

Although I was angry, I decided not to show it — for foolishness is not bravery — and I wanted to make this man my friend. We all know that if you cannot flatter a man for his accomplishments, praise him for those of his sons, and if he is childless for those of his people.

"Damascus is a great city, I am told; even greater than Caesarea is."

The robber laughed and said with contempt, "Caesarea was built by King Herod. Damascus stood with walls and towers when the Greeks only tended sheep."

"This I have heard, too; and I have never understood why the Roman governor lives in Antioch and not in Damascus."

The bandit lifted his head and looked towards the horizon; he was imagining his native city. "Judean dog," he began, but there was no curse in his tone. "To Damascus comes everyone. No language is spoken in the world that you cannot hear in the marketplace there. The figs that grow there are bigger than a man's hand and sweeter than any others. The plums have the color of precious stones, which you can buy from the country at the end of the world. The wine is so strong that it makes heroes out of cowards."

'His heart is sick for his home,' I thought. 'He wants to be with his own people again.' Excitedly, I wondered how loyal he could be to the "King of Samaria." The Syrian was frowning now. "I know about the wine," I said eagerly. "My father is a wine merchant and he buys much wine from Damascus."

My guard turned to look at me carefully. I was his prisoner and a prisoner is powerless; but suddenly, I could see in his expression that he was remembering the hundred gold pieces that I was worth.

"Bring the Judean to the 'king'; he wants to talk with him."

My guard glanced up at the man and grimaced. He was one of the leaders; he, too, rode on horseback. He grunted as he turned from us.

"He is from beyond the sea," my guard mumbled. "I think he is a Greek." I understood from his tone that a Greek had much in common with a "Judean dog."

It was difficult for me to get up because my hands were tied behind my back. At my first attempt I fell backwards, which made my guard laugh; but, to my surprise, when I tried to get up again, he helped me.

The "king" sat with his "court" in a circle around him. When I came, a place was made for me opposite him; but otherwise, no notice was taken of my arrival. I knew that I had been brought to amuse them. They had eaten and were drinking now, though none appeared drunk. The man who had ordered me to be brought sat on the right of the "king"; on his left sat a boy of my own age, who kept glancing at me when he thought I was looking in another direction. One of the bandits had the fine features of a Saracen, those people who wander from place to place in the Arabian desert. The rest of the bandits had such brutish faces that I thought, 'They belong to no people; they are animals who have disguised themselves as human beings by putting on clothes.'

"Give the prisoner some wine," the "king" ordered, and a bowl was placed in front of my crossed legs. "Drink, Judean. This is Samarian wine and you may find it bitter for a Judean tongue."

"My hands are bound behind me. How can I drink?" I heard rough laughter. A hand pushed my neck forward; my head struck the bowl as I fell.

"The Judean does not like Samarian wine, he spills it onto the ground like Eleazar spilled Samarian blood."

With great difficulty, which amused the onlookers, I lifted myself to my knees. "Fill up the bowl!" It was again placed before me. I knew what was expected; I was to drink from it as an animal.

"Drink! Drink!" the shouts came from all around me.

They had not brought me here to kill me but to taunt me. "To drink like an animal does not make you into one," I said but I did not look at their faces. I bent my head down towards the bowl. The wine was bitter, more like vinegar than wine; but I drank until the bowl was empty. They laughed loudly, for the last swallows of the wine I had lapped like a dog.

"How do you like the wine of Samaria?" the "king" asked threateningly.

I answered that it was strong and the "king" called for the bowl to be filled up again. Six times I emptied the bowl; my hair and clothes were wet. As the seventh was placed before me, I fell forward and could not get up. My last memory of that evening was seeing the face of the Syrian guard near mine; perhaps he was bending down to pick me up.

When I awoke in the morning, my head ached, my mouth felt dirty, and my tongue was swollen. 'So this is what it is like to be drunk,' I thought and I promised myself that I would never be so again. Several times I lifted my head but I made no real effort to get up. I slept and woke again. Something was itching me. I looked down at myself: I was not wearing my own clothes and my feet were bare. I had on the dirty rags that the poorest shepherds wore. My own robes had been sewn by the women in my father's house and had been of the finest linen. For the first time since my capture I felt the fear of hopelessness. More terrible than my clothes having been taken from me was the thought that the robbers had undressed me while I slept.

"Well, Judean . . . Get up. Now you know how the wine of Samaria tastes: bitter on the tongue when you drink it and heavy on the head the day after." The man from Damascus was sitting near me, leaning against a packsaddle.

"Who took my clothes?" I was moving my fingers as rapidly as I could, for my hands were numb within their bonds; but it was a long time before they began to tingle and then they started to hurt.

"The boy took them. The boy who sat next to the chief. Not that he did it himself. He would not dare to do anything himself. Some of the others undressed you but he got your clothes. I carried you back here as naked as you came into the world."

I shuddered and felt ashamed. "But I have clothes on now."

"Those I got for you. They would have left you naked."

"Thank you," I said and then as I realized how miserable and defenseless I would have been without these rags, I repeated, "Thank you . . . Thank you." The Syrian laughed good-naturedly. "Who is the 'king'?" I asked.

"A shepherd from Samaria, who started his life as king by taking his master's flock into the Galilee and selling it. He is a drunken, stupid dog and before the year is out, he will be food for the vultures."

"Why do you follow him?" I asked.

He thought a long time before he answered. "Most men are nothing. You will learn that if you live long enough; but that doesn't matter if they have never seen their reflection in a mirror. Then they don't know that they are nothing."

"And the 'king' hasn't stolen any mirror yet, so he doesn't know that he is nothing."

"If he had every mirror in Caesarea, he would learn nothing about himself. The reflection in polished metal tells only what eyes see. What am I? A mule tender from Damascus, the kind of man that steps aside on the road when your father's caravan passes. I know what I am and even my dreams stink of mules."

I smiled. Had my hands not been tied, I would have reached out to touch the Syrian's hand. Perhaps it is just as well that I could not, for he might not have understood; besides, I am not sure that I was capable of doing it.

The robbers began to load their mules and saddle their horses; we were to start for some new resting place. I was hungry and thirsty; I also wanted to ask for a pair of sandals; I was not used to walking barefooted. I was looking down at my feet; my guard followed my gaze and grinned. A few minutes later, he gave me a pair of sandals; they were clumsily cut and I think they were a pair of his own. As I could not use my hands, he had to tie them on my feet. When he was finished he helped me up. It felt strange to stand. I was dizzy and though I had promised myself to ask for nothing more, I did ask for water. He held his waterbag up to my lips. The water was not fresh but I drank it eagerly.

The "King of Samaria" was already in his saddle. Next to him was the boy who was wearing my clothes. He was mounting his horse. When he noticed me, he laughed and stroked his clothes with his hand. I kept staring at him to show my contempt. This was very foolish; but then, one is not always wise.

The "king" shouted and those on horseback started to ride. They were coming in our direction. My guard was saddling one of the mules. I stepped backwards; the leader passed close by me. The boy was a distance behind him. Suddenly I realized that he was going to try to run me down. For a moment I was held fast by the sound of the hoofs and the sight of his face.

It is difficult to run with your hands tied behind you and at any moment I expected to fall and be trampled to death. To the right of me, I saw a clump of briars almost my own height. I pressed myself against the bushes. The horse veered. The boy held the reins tightly and rode on; then he turned in his saddle and stuck out his tongue. My shoulders and arms were scratched by thorns. It was not a terrible pain but smarting and sharp; in spite of myself, my eyes filled with tears.

FREE AGAIN! | 7

THE BANDITS now marched south, keeping out of sight of Megiddo and its Roman garrison. No one seemed to care about me. At noon a short rest was called and each man began to eat the food he had left over from the morning meal. My guard sat a distance away from me. I was lying down. Suddenly he was standing over me; he dropped a large piece of bread onto my chest, then motioned for me to turn over. The bread fell on the earth, but I hardly noticed for the Syrian was untying my hands, and this was a greater blessing than food.

My hands were so weak and numb that I could not

pick up the bread. My guard told me to rub them first against the rough wool of my clothes and then against each other. It was not before the end of our rest that they felt normal again.

The ability to think, to reflect, to step aside from yourself, is a curse when you are among other children. I remember many times when the feeling of loneliness could come over me at play, and I would watch the eager faces of the other children as if they were reproaching me. But now I learned that it is true what is said about a coin having two sides, for the only way to conquer fear is by thought.

'I must escape.' By saying this simple sentence to myself, I felt an immense relief, as if I were free already. When the guard tied my hands again, I held them a little apart, so that the thongs would not be so tight. The Syrian laughed, "Judean, I am no fool, though I walk in the footsteps of one." But he did not tie my hands tightly and I felt certain that later I would be able to loosen the leather strips.

"Where are we going?" I asked my guard. The sun was moving towards the horizon and soon the chill of evening would come.

"Our leader comes from a village near the city of Samaria, a village that the people of Judea once destroyed."

"Wasn't it built up again by Herod the Great?"

The Syrian nodded and then shrugged his shoulders. "That Herod of yours was a madman. He killed his own family, his own children! While he was king, the people of Judea cursed him and said that he was not a Jew. Now that he is dead long enough for the ants to have eaten his carcass, you praise him."

Out of the corner of my eye, I looked at the man from Damascus. He was so clever. Why did he live among bandits risking his life for nothing? "People's sins die with their bodies; their accomplishments live longer."

"Judean, don't you know that virtue, not accomplishment, is the opposite of weakness? And while a man is living, we condemn his faults because we have the same faults ourselves . . . When he is dead, we forgive him for the same reason."

"But Herod did have virtues," I argued.

"You condemn a man for his weaknesses and you hate him for his virtues; that is why no man is virtuous while he lives. When he is dead it does not matter." The Syrian grunted. "A dead man is nothing."

The landscape was hilly now. 'Soon we will camp,' I told myself, 'and then during the night I shall escape.' But I feared that I might be called to amuse the bandits again as I had been the night before. I thought of the boy: he was not only stupid but evil as well. I caught up with the Syrian who was a few steps ahead of me, and asked him about the boy.

"He will make the vultures vomit," he said. When I asked him why, my guard shook his head and would say no more.

It was almost dusk when we saw a part of a division of Roman cavalry riding towards us. There were more than a hundred well-armed men and the bandits had no chance against them. As they approached us in perfect formation, their captain called out first in Greek then in Aramaic for the bandits to put down their weapons and seek Roman mercy.

The "King of Samaria" screamed back at him, in Aramaic, "Roman mercy! When have the Romans ever shown mercy?" He let loose the bridle and kicked his horse. It broke into a gallop. Followed by the other of the robbers who were on horseback, he fled south towards Samaria. The bandits who were on foot began to run in all directions. Their only hope of safety was that the Romans could not follow all of them at once, and a few would have the luck to escape.

The Syrian grabbed one of my arms and started running. I could not run as fast as he, and he was half dragging me. Wisely, he chose to run up a hill, for it was very rocky, the kind a horse does not like to climb. I stumbled and fell, but the Syrian ran on.

A horse galloped past me. I caught a glimpse of the Syrian; he had almost reached the top of the hill. He turned around and cried out. The rider had caught up with him. With his full strength the Roman soldier plunged his sword downward into the Syrian's neck; then he rode on. I saw the Syrian lift his hands to his neck. The blood was spouting from it as I have seen water rush from the fountain in the marketplace in Tyre. He fell backwards and his head struck a stone.

All this I saw without lifting my head. Blood was running from a cut on my cheek. I expected any moment to be killed by a sword or a spear; yet I worked my hands round, trying to get them free. Finally, the strip on my left hand was loosened and I pulled it free of my right. I felt my cheek; the cut was not deep.

I lay there as motionless as I could. Many times I heard horses' hoofs and voices near me. My heart beat so loudly that I feared it would burst. It was almost dark when I heard the roar of hundreds of hoofs. The Romans were reassembling. I turned my head. They were re-forming in a plain quite a distance away. Still I did not dare sit up. From the south a group of cavalrymen were approaching; yet even in the failing light I could make out the riderless horses. Among them was the white horse of the "King of Samaria"; his lifeless body had been flung across the horse's back, his scarlet coat trailed on the ground. I thought two of the other horses carried bodies, but I could not be sure.

The soldiers started to ride in the direction of Megiddo. Horses and men became one shadow as they moved into the darkness. I stood up and slowly walked towards the top of the hill where the Syrian had fallen. As my hands had been lamed by the rope, so now my brain was bound by what had happened. Although I knew that the Syrian was dead, I started to talk with him. I touched his face. Now I would never hear his story. He would never tell me why he had joined the bandits. The towers of Damascus had fallen: faults and virtues had become one.

I sat beside the dead Syrian all night. I don't know why, for surely I should have run away. When I had first seen the Romans, for one happy moment I had thought that I could demand their protection. But how would the soldiers know that I spoke the truth, when I said that I was not one of the bandits? How could I be sure that they had been sent out to find the "King of Samaria," with the knowledge that he had taken me with him for ransom? My clothes were rags; how could I be the son of a rich merchant from Tyre?

The night was cold. In the far distance I saw a fire, probably where the soldiers had camped for the night. The sight of the fire made my loneliness greater, the darkness darker. A dog howled — or was it a jackal or a wolf? A jackal can smell the blood of the dead. Some say that they are the souls of robbers, who cannot rest after death.

When morning came, my body was stiff with cold. I jumped up and down to get warm, hitting my shoulders with my hands as I swung my arms around myself. Below me in every direction I could see the corpses of the bandits. There were flocks of buzzards and other birds of prey. The soldiers were gone. They must have broken camp before I awoke; or maybe it had not been their fire I had seen.

I looked down at the Syrian's face with its eyes staring upwards towards the sky. I heard the buzzards before I saw them; one of them was beating the air with its wings. They were two and they were only a few paces away. I took a stone and threw it at them. They flew a very short distance and landed again. I hate that bird; its yellow, arrogant eyes seem to know no fear.

It was because of the birds that I buried the Syrian — not that I could dig him a grave; the ground was too hard for that. I collected stones, while the buzzards watched; and then, as if they understood what I was preparing to do, they spread their wings and flew away.

When I had covered the Syrian with stones, I lingered, staring at his grave. I wanted to say something, recite a prayer; but I did not know his gods and how could I say the Prayer for the Dead over a gentile. I stood up to walk away; and then — though I don't know why — I spoke: "*'Hear, O Israel, the Lord is Our God, the Lord is One.'*"

THROUGH SAMARIA | 8

THE PLACE where the soldiers had killed the bandits was a day's march from Caesarea. In Caesarea my father had friends and a message would be sent to him that I was well. In Caesarea I would be fed, I could wash and again be clothed in material that was soft against the skin. But I did not return to Caesarea, I walked south through Samaria towards Judea, in the direction of Jerusalem.

In so few days, so much had changed. I was no longer the same David: the David who had lived in Tyre, the rich merchant's son whom everyone knew.

Oh, I was he, too, as the snake is still the snake though it has shed its skin. But I was also the Judean dog, the prisoner with his hands tied behind him. The world was no longer safe and returning to my father's table would not have made it so. These were all thoughts; and thoughts are like the wind that whips the waves, where they come from no one knows.

When I walked south, I turned my back on my mother and my father, who had always been kind to me. I did not think of their days that would be spent listening to every traveler in the hope that a stray word would lead to news that I was alive, nor of their restless nights when their thoughts would circle endlessly around the same fears. I wanted to go to Jerusalem to see the Temple. I had been told that it had been destroyed; but it drew me towards it, as if the walls that still stood in my mind and heart needed to become ruins.

I did not follow any roads, only paths, and I skirted all villages and towns. I was in Samaria and I was a Jew. Between the Samaritans and the Jews there is no peace. Although we worship the same God, the Samaritans recognize only the Five Books of Moses as holy. They have built their own temple on Mount Gerizim. One of Herod's wives was a Samaritan woman, but Herod kept only Herod's law.

By late afternoon I was terribly hungry, but worse than that I was thirsty. Just outside a village I saw a well that was attended by a boy; he looked a year or two years younger than myself. I could offer him no payment, but he drew water for me and let me drink. I thanked the boy. He explained that his father owned the well.

I should have walked on for a well is as attractive to men as flowers are to bees. But I was tired and I stayed. I hoped, too, that the boy would offer me something to eat. When he asked me where I came from, I pointed north; and when he asked me where I was going, I shrugged my shoulders.

The boy picked up a stone, put it in a sling, and threw it. I watched it ascend into the sky like a bird, then lose speed as it came to the highest point in the arch. For a moment it appeared almost to stand still before it plunged to the earth.

'He is stronger than I am,' I thought; and I envied him his ability with the sling.

I picked up a stone and the boy handed me the sling. When I was prepared to cast it, it fell from the small patch of leather. The boy laughed and picked up my stone. He shook his head. Quickly he found another and showed it to me. It was the same size as mine had been but it was more nearly round and heavier. He put the pebble in his sling and threw it. This time the arch was lower but the stone flew further than before.

I wanted to learn how to use the sling, but the boy did not offer it to me again. He placed one of his hands next to mine. My fingers were long and thin; his were short but his hand was much broader. He turned my hand over and compared the palm to his own; the skin of his palm was thick from work.

"You are not a slave who has run away," he said.

The defenseless always have to think quickly, for all their actions are governed by their weakness. I told the boy who I was, how I had been captured by the bandits, and how the bandits had been killed by the Roman soldiers. As I came to the end of the story my gaze did not leave his face. I was a Jew. He might run to the village and tell about me. I had to be prepared to run even if he only wished to fight with me himself.

When I stopped speaking, the boy continued to look at me. "Did they have horses?" he asked excitedly. "What color were they?"

"There was one white one," I said. I could only remember the color of the "King of Samaria's" horse. I had paid no attention to any of the others.

"He wore a scarlet cape, their leader. He stole my father's horse," the boy explained. "He plundered this village not long ago." He was silent for a moment, then he said, "I will tell my father. Do you think the Romans would give the horse back to him?"

"I don't know," I said.

"They wouldn't!" he exclaimed angrily; then he said to me kindly, "You are hungry." From the leather bag that leaned against the well, he took out some bread and a small piece of cheese.

There was no more than one mouthful of cheese and I swallowed it quickly. I was just about to shove the bread into my mouth, when the boy put his hand on mine. "Eat more slowly or you will get sick. You have never felt hunger before, I can see that. You may have spoken the truth when you say that your father is rich. When one has hungered long, one should eat slowly, small bits at a time. My father says that the stomach of the hungry is like a poor man. If you give a poor man a lot of gold, he will spend it foolishly and get nothing out of it; but if you give him a single large, silver coin, he will act wisely."

I broke the bread into pieces. It was hard; it must have been baked several days before. "Eat half of it now," he warned, "and save the other half for the morning."

The boy was younger than I, and he was giving me good advice. "Thank you for the food," I muttered. To show him that I was not always so foolish, I added, "When you are hungry, you are like an animal, and think with your stomach instead of your head."

He laughed, and his laughter was sweet for his voice had not yet changed. "You are, indeed, a rich man's son for you know nothing of animals. They are all different. The sheep will eat until its belly blows up as a skin does from fermenting wine; but a horse that is hungry will wait and eat only a little at a time."

I took a small bite of the bread and chewed it slowly. The boy nodded approvingly; then he looked at the horizon. The sun was just above it. "Tomorrow my brother will come to the well. He is older and thinks himself a man, so do not come here tomorrow." He put the wooden cover over the opening of the well and rolled up the rope that he had used to lower the copper bucket. But I did not get up from the stone trough used for watering the animals, for I didn't want the boy to leave. I glanced at the sky; I knew that he soon would have to go home. As I looked at the sun, it occurred to me that today must be the Sabbath. Samaritans keep the Sabbath as the Jews do; and I asked the boy why he had come to the well.

He grinned. "Yesterday was the Sabbath; if you had come then you would have found the well unguarded."

"Yesterday!" I said unbelievingly. How could a day disappear like an hour?

It had been on the Sabbath then that the bandits had been killed, and we had traveled all day contrary to the Law.

"I must go."

The boy's voice interrupted my thoughts. "Thank you for the food and the water," I said.

The boy looked down at the ground, as if to say, 'It was nothing.' He walked ten paces then he turned around and stared at me. He raised his hand in a kind of salute before he turned again and walked away.

I sat near the well and watched his figure become smaller and smaller until it disappeared. Suddenly the evening became darker. At home, in Tyre, lamps would soon be lit and the table prepared for supper. The remembering of the familiar made the landscape seem unfriendly. At that moment I would have been glad to be home. Some of the stars were already visible. I watched the western sky until the last glow from the sun was gone; then I started walking again, south towards Jerusalem.

DARKNESS AND SILENCE blot out the world, only knowledge and memory tell you that it exists. All night I walked, for I feared if I sat down I would recall all the tales told to me when I was a child about demons. In darkness you can fall over an unseen stone and the bark of a dog sends fright running through you. I walked in the direction that I thought would lead me to Jerusalem, but how could I know where I was going in the darkness? I could not read the stars the way the people of the desert can; they can walk in the endless sand as I walked the streets of Tyre.

At dawn, I rested. I had no thought of sleeping and

yet sleep came, and with it, curious dreams: I was in my father's house; but my father was not my father, nor was his house in Tyre. It was a strange town and I could not recognize my father's face — not that he looked like anyone else but he had no features. He wore his Sabbath clothes and yet it was not the Sabbath for in the kitchen they were baking bread. He did not speak to me and when I approached him he disappeared. I called him and ran from the house. The street was one I did not know, and when I turned to look back at my father's house, it was no longer there. I saw a marketplace, but it was not the marketplace of Tyre. I walked among the stalls; the people attending them had faces like my father's: featureless. At last I came to the stall of a man who was selling copperware. This man had a face. He laughed and beckoned to me with his finger. I started towards him. I felt afraid, I wanted to run away but I could not. The man's face was dark, tanned by the sun; his nose was large and curved; his eyes were black. He was a handsome man; he was dressed in blue garments. When I reached the stall and stood before him, he took from among the pots a dagger, which he held out to me. I shook my head, I did not want it; but his eyes commanded me to take it. The handle was of silver: two intertwined snakes, whose eyes were four small rubies. It was a costly weapon meant to be worn by a prince. It fell from my hand and hit the ground.

I woke up; but so real had the dream been that I

searched the ground on either side of me for the dagger.

A small stone hit my back. I turned. Behind me stood four children. The oldest was my own size; two of the others were much younger; the third was small of stature but I could not guess his age for his face had the expression of a grown man. I was still staring at this boy when the biggest one asked me menacingly, "Who are you, stranger?" In his uplifted hand, he held a stone larger than the one he had thrown.

'Where am I?' I asked myself silently. 'Still in Samaria, or have I passed into Judea?' Aloud, I said, "I am a traveler."

"Are you a Samaritan? Or are you a Greek?" The way the name Samaritan was pronounced convinced me that I was in Judea.

"I am from Tyre. I am a Keeper of the Law. My name is David ben Joseph and I am a Pharisee."

The boy let his arm fall to his side; but he did not throw the rock away. "How do we know that you speak the truth?"

"Why should I lie?" I countered, knowing full well that four against one was a very good reason to lie.

"We are followers of Eleazar ben Dinai, ruler of Judea!"

I could not help laughing: Was Eleazar ben Dinai to haunt me as an ancestor's sin? "Eleazar is dead, how can he have followers?"

"He was my uncle," the oldest boy said proudly. "All of Samaria feared him!"

"Not only all of Samaria," I said. Eleazar ben Dinai had been feared in Judea as well; for twenty years he had made the roads unsafe. He had killed so many people that he was also called Eleazar ben Harazhan, which means "the murderer." He had claimed that he wanted to free the Jews from Roman rule, but I think that Joseph ben Matthias was right when he called him a thief and cutthroat, too ignorant to know the Torah, but cunning enough to misuse it.

"I shall revenge him!" The nephew of Eleazar ben Dinai looked at me with hatred in his eyes.

"He was killed in Rome many years ago," I argued. "Long before this war began." It seemed strange to hear anyone speak of revenge now, when Jerusalem had fallen and a Jew was like the dead leaf that is blown by the winds.

"It was a Samaritan who betrayed him!"

"He is a Samaritan!" The youngest boy sang the words with joy and threw a stone at me, but he missed his mark. It fell harmlessly at the side of me.

" 'A stranger who walks through your land and does not harm you, his life is holy unto you and you must protect him. If you raise your hand against the defenseless, God will wither your arm.' " I had spoken in the language of the Torah and my words had frightened the boy. Though he had not understood them, he recognized them as words spoken by priests and learned men.

"Let him be," the big boy commanded; and now he

himself let the stone he had kept in his hand fall to the ground. "Have you any food?"

For the first time, I noticed how pitifully thin the children were.

"We have not eaten in two days," one of them said.

"You had better return to Jerusalem and speak to one of the priests or one of the elders, and a home will be found for you."

"There is no food in Jerusalem!" the biggest boy screamed at me, and on the faces of the other children, I saw that he spoke the truth.

"And is there food here?" I asked and with a wave of my arm took in the hills behind us. The few bushes were dried yellow by the constant sun of summer and early autumn. My words made an impression on the younger children. The oldest one looked at me with contempt, and the other, whose age I could not guess, had no expression to belie his thoughts. "I am going to Jerusalem; come with me. If there is no food in Jerusalem, then we can travel to some other city where there live people who keep the Law."

The youngest boy said, "My name is Daniel."

"Won't you come with me, Daniel," I said gently.

A rock hit my shoulder. The pain was sharp. I touched the shoulder with my hand and moved it cautiously. I heard the oldest boy's laughter; I turned, he was bending down to pick up another rock. I jumped on him. My attack surprised him and he sprawled out on the ground. I flung myself on top of him and hit him in the face. If I were to beat him, I must do it quickly before the other children gained enough courage to help him. Four times I hit his face with my fists. When his nose started bleeding I stood up. He did not move. He was crying and the tears mixed with blood. The hatred in his eyes was terrible for me to look at, for I did not understand it; but I dared not take my gaze from him for fear he would find another rock. Finally, he got up and started to run away. He had not run far when he turned to face me.

"You keep them. They are children, I would have left them."

"They are children and it was wrong of you to have taken them with you," I said slowly. I was trying to think of some argument to persuade him to go back to Jerusalem with me.

Swiftly his hand reached down for a rock. "I'll throw it if you come nearer!"

"I am a stranger from Tyre. Why don't you help me to take the children back to Jerusalem? There you can find other boys your own age to be your followers." Suddenly I realized that as I spoke I had been slowly walking towards him.

He laughed and I turned around to see the expressions on the others' faces. This time the rock hit my leg and stunned me. Fear-filled as he was, he had already started to run away. I did not try to pursue him; my leg was bleeding and it hurt badly.

"In the city, they caught him stealing and the soldiers whipped him," the boy whose age I could not guess explained. His tone was cold and expressionless as the voice you have heard in a dream.

"Will you come with me?"

Daniel muttered, "Yes." The others only nodded.

SAUL'S STORY | 10

We did not walk as far as Jerusalem that day, but we spent the night in the hills not far from the city. These hills are high, but I would not call them mountains. They are softly rounded, as if God had patted them into shape as I used to the sand houses that I made on the beach near Tyre. Before the siege, they had been covered by great forests; but now almost all of the tall trees were cut down. The branches of the smaller trees had been torn off and many of the saplings uprooted. This the Roman soldiers, to whom these hills were a strange country, had done. It was sad in the same way that a forest destroyed by fire is. The children did not seem to notice, for they had suffered so much that the tragedy of a broken tree could not reach them.

At noon we had eaten. We had gone to a farm. At first the farmer had given us nothing. He said that he was poor and that the soldiers had robbed him of everything. Daniel, the youngest boy, began to cry; but tears could not move this man, for he had grown used to suffering. He told us gruffly to go away; and angrily, I shouted at him the words from the Torah:

" '*When thou cuttest down the harvest in thy field, and thou hast forgotten a sheaf in the field, thou shalt not go again to fetch it: it shall be for the fatherless!*' "

The man gazed at me with narrowed eyes, as if he were weighing an ox. 'He is afraid,' I thought, 'for he believes in the Law. And what man has not taken up from the ground the olives meant for the poor and put them in his press?'

"The sheaves are gone now," I continued in Hebrew. "And only in the seasons do the olives fall from the tree; but the poor and the fatherless must also live when the fields are barren. '*Should we not see the outstretched hand of the beggar and forget that once we were slaves in Egypt, then God will see the empty hand and God will remember our bondage.*' "

My words made the impression that I had hoped, and grudgingly he told us to wait. Our people are different from the Greeks, the Romans, and the other gentile people whom we live among, in that we respect learning above all other accomplishments. The Romans and the Greeks will go to see two men fight each other, or pride themselves on the swiftness with which they can run; but we Jews love a man who can talk well of things beyond us. As often as not we honor fools who have learned the Torah by heart. Such fellows are in my mind as useless as runners or fighters, but when you praise the runner, you are also praising the sport, in which an animal can excel; and when you crown the fool who recites from the Torah, you are paying homage to the Words of God.

The farmer gave us a loaf of bread, some goat cheese, and a handful of olives. I shared the food and admonished the children to eat slowly; but little Daniel ate his food so fast that he was finished before any of the rest of us. While we rested I thought about the farmer. I felt no gratitude towards him; he had not given us food because he had felt sorry for us but because he had been afraid. Yet a moment later I asked myself, 'Is it not right to fear God?' I looked at the children. Though they had not eaten much, they were contented. Suddenly, without knowing why, I was angry: angry at the farmer and the children. I leapt to my feet and ordered them to get up, though I knew that they were still tired, especially Daniel.

I did not let them rest until night started creeping into the valleys and only on the hilltops was there light. Near Jerusalem the first rains of autumn had come and the night was bitterly cold. We sat close together so that we could draw warmth from each other. Although we were weary we could not sleep because of the cold; and I feared that the night would be long.

I had heard that all of the city was in ruins and I asked the children if it were true, for I could not believe it.

"Most of the city has been burned," Saul said in that emotionless tone that always made me give him my full attention, even when he spoke of meaningless things, and kept me from asking him anything about himself, even his age. "The soldiers put fire to it. The silver on the doors of the Temple melted." Saul's voice came out of the darkness. "I was with my parents in the Upper City, the last part to fall. The soldiers killed my father and my brother. They took my sister away . . . They did not kill my mother because she had already died two days before.

"We had had no food for a month in the Upper City and many people had died. My mother had given birth to a girl. The girl lived only a few days . . . There was no food, so my mother let my little brother suckle. My brother was four years old."

A bat or a bird flew past. Daniel moved closer to me. For his sake, I wanted to ask Saul to stop talking but I could not.

"When the soldiers first came into the city, they killed everyone: old people and children alike. They said it was the order of Titus. I saw Titus once; his horse was white and covered with a scarlet cloth that he had stolen from the Temple. My father had defended the city with the others."

For a while Saul said nothing, then he began again as if there had been no pause. "But my brother was only four years old."

I put my arm around Daniel as I wondered what he might have seen.

"Four years old and the soldier killed him with his sword. I saw it, I was hiding under a bed. I thought the soldier would drag me out and kill me, too, but our house was too poor; after he killed my brother he ran out. They were mad for gold. They went from one house to the other. They could not believe that we were poor. Some of the people they beat and wounded with their swords, to make them tell where their gold was. They screamed that they had none. But the soldiers did not believe them because they had seen the treasures of the Temple.

"For two days they were wild like winter-starved wolves; then they stopped killing. My sister and I had been in the cellar of our house three days when they found us. They took us to their camp, where we were to be sold as slaves. But there were so many people to sell and so few to buy: a grown man sold for a few small silver coins. Many of them Titus bought, himself; they were to be shipped to Egypt. I was one of them, but I ran away. My sister was bought by an officer. I have not seen her since."

Daniel had fallen asleep. The other boy, whose name was Samuel, was crying; but when Saul finished he started speaking through his tears, "I was not at home when the soldiers came. I was in the street. I had been hungry and there was nothing to eat at home. A crowd of people came running down the street; the soldiers were chasing them. I started to run with them; but then I fell and they stepped on me. I crawled to the wall of a house. It hurt so terribly . . . all over. The soldiers didn't touch me. Maybe they thought I was dead, for there were many dead in the streets. I lay there until it was dark, then I went home. Our house had been burned. Someone told me that the soldiers had killed them all." Samuel ceased talking but not crying, but now he cried softly until Saul told him to stop.

I did not say anything. The stars were out and I looked up at them. I remembered that my father had said to me once, when I had feigned sickness because I did not want to go to my Greek teacher: "You must study . . . '*You must incline your ear to wisdom and apply your heart to understanding.*' " I had read the story of the Greeks who set out to punish the city of Troy. In the end it said that they had razed that city to the ground. Had it been more than words to me, or even to my teacher?

Finally, we fell asleep; but before the sun rose we were awakened by the cold. We sat shivering, waiting for the light of dawn. When it came at last, like a white fog in the darkness, and we could see each others' faces, we stood up to continue our journey to Jerusalem.

JERUSALEM | 11

"THEY ARE breaking down the walls," Samuel said. Even from afar the destruction of the city was plainly to be seen.

"It is an order of Titus," Saul explained. We were standing on the crest of a hill from which we could see Jerusalem.

"The towers are still there, but where is the Temple?" I knew that the Temple had been destroyed but I had expected to see sections of the walls and the colonnades still standing.

"Some of the walls caved in during the fire. Titus

ordered all that were still standing after the fire to be torn down."

I glanced at Saul to try to read his face, but I could not guess his thoughts; and I had to turn away so that he would not see that I was crying. A sentence from one of the songs came to me: "*Pray for the peace of Jerusalem, they shall prosper that love thee.*" My tears of sorrow became tears of rage! Many of the people who had died in the city had come for the Passover festival: had they not come because they loved Jerusalem and the Temple? Who had cared about them? Had God cared? What did it mean to be His People, when we were to be destroyed? What did it matter to be a Keeper of the Law, when the Law counted for no one but us?

"Look," Saul pointed towards a camp that was set out in a square. There were hundreds of tents and in the center was an open square. "That's where the Romans live, outside the city."

"How many are there?" I asked.

Saul shrugged his shoulders, but Samuel said, "More than a hundred thousand." A short distance from the first I made out a second camp.

"Let's go on," Saul said irritably.

The closer we came to the city, the more we could see of the destruction. I had hoped to be able to find some of my father's friends from whom to get help for myself and the children. But now, as we approached the first houses, I began to doubt; for surely, those who could have must have fled, and those who remained needed help themselves. In the Lower City not a door was left on any house. They had been taken by the Romans to build the wooden towers for scaling the Temple walls. As we passed, we could see into the houses. Many had been set on fire and the roofs had fallen in, so that often as not what from the outside looked like a house was, in reality, no more than the shell of a ruin. The people in the streets averted each others' glances. Each had so much grief within himself that he needed not to be reminded of his neighbors'.

Everywhere there were soldiers. In some places booths had been opened where food was being sold. In one they were roasting a lamb. We stood and watched. Near us was an old woman; she, too, was smelling the roast with no hope of tasting it. I looked at the owner, but his face was not as inviting as his meats, and I walked on. Daniel stayed behind. We called to him; and when he finally came his face had such an odd expression that we all laughed.

The house that I was seeking, where I had stayed with my father, was in the Upper City. This is the oldest part of Jerusalem and it was the last to fall. The Lower City and the New City near Herod's Wall had been heavily damaged; but the Upper City had been systematically destroyed. Here the soldiers had murdered most of the population; and here in the sewers the last defenders had died. The houses were empty. All of them had been looted and what had been left behind of furnishings had been broken or torn.

It took me a long time to find the house of my father's friend — and perhaps I never did find it, but only a house that resembled it. I remembered that over the main entrance there had been a bunch of grapes, carved in stone, and that in the courtyard there had been a small fountain. There were no portals. The big wooden doors had been broken off at the hinges; one was lying on the ground, the other was leaning against the wall. We stepped into the courtyard. It seemed smaller than I recalled, but there was a fountain, though no water came from it. The house had been burned and pieces of the roof littered the courtyard. Already it had taken on the desolation of a ruin and I could not imagine that once — so short a time ago — it had been the dwelling of a rich merchant.

The living quarters had been on one side of the courtyard and opposite them, in the direction of the street, had been the entrance. On one of the remaining sides of the courtyard had been a stable, and on the other, a warehouse. The stable and the warehouse were still there. The doors had been wrenched off as the main gate had been, but they had not been burned, though in one corner the wall of the warehouse was charred.

It was growing dark. I called out loudly, "Shalom, Asher ben Ezra . . . Shalom." No one answered.

"Shalom. Is this the house of Asher ben Ezra?" There was no reply.

We looked through the doorway of the warehouse; it was dark inside and we dared not enter. I crossed to the stable. It, too, appeared empty. Although the animals were gone, the smell of donkeys and horses remained. It was a friendly smell and I stepped inside.

I saw the light from the embers immediately, even before I smelled the smoke. At the far end of the stable, someone had built a fire not long before. "Shalom," I called out. "I am David ben Joseph of Tyre and I am looking for Asher ben Ezra, who is the master of this house."

Still no one answered. Cautiously, I walked up to the fire. I was certain that I was not alone. "Shalom!" I called louder. I heard the children enter the stable. "My name is David ben Joseph. My father is called Joseph ben Noah and is a merchant in Tyre. I am looking for Asher ben Ezra!"

From somewhere in the darkness, laughter answered me: the laughter of an old man or woman who no longer could cry and therefore laughed.

Daniel pressed himself close to me. I reached out and touched Samuel's shoulder. "They are but children. We shall do you no harm."

In the corner at a distance from the fire, I saw a shadow move. Dragging Daniel with me, I made my way to the dying fire. Samuel and Saul followed us. I came so close to it that my eyes smarted from the smoke. In the dim glow whoever it was could not help seeing us and he would realize that I had spoken the truth. I had thought that this would calm his fears, but now there came a scream, "Go away! Go away!" I stepped back.

"We are staying here for the night, grandfather. We shall do you no harm . . . You will be cold in your corner, so you might as well come over here and get warm near the fire."

He had spoken roughly and I, being used to speaking respectfully to the old, was surprised. Saul already was busy collecting bits of twigs and feeding them to the fire. "He is frightened, the old one," Saul remarked without turning to look at me. "After the fall of the city, many of the children were parentless and all of them were hungry. They banded together. They stole, if they could find anything. I believe that they killed some of the old people. Whenever they could, the Roman soldiers caught them. They had the children whipped and a couple of them were crucified."

I could not take my eyes from Saul as he worked. I wondered whether he, too, had been in one of these gangs.

As if I had spoken, he said, "I was never caught. But I never belonged to any band. I found Joseph — the boy who was with us and whom you hit — after he had been whipped. He couldn't walk. I think the soldiers left him to die; but he had bragged that he had killed two people for the sake of a hen. I think he was lying; but he was crazy."

Saul had rekindled the fire and now a bright flame lighted up his face. "Not that he couldn't have committed murder, for he was mad. Have you ever seen a dog that has gotten the madness? It will attack a man or a horse, even though in size it couldn't fight a tomcat. That is the way Joseph was mad; and as those dogs who have the madness are stoned to death, so Joseph will die." Saul's tone never left any doubt that his words came from experience: from what he had seen, if not from what he himself had done. Until now the fears I had known had been fear of danger, of pain, of death; but when Saul spoke I knew another fear which made me shiver, though I knew not its name.

Daniel pulled at my arm. The old man was approaching the fire. His body was barely covered by the rags he wore; he looked like a skeleton. When he opened his mouth, I saw that he had no teeth. "Up the street . . . Up the street, there is food." His eyes shone as a miser's when he talks of gold.

"What do you mean, grandfather?" I asked, trying to imitate Saul's way of speaking.

"You will have to kill them," the old man croaked, "for they won't give anything away."

In disgust, I looked away from the old man who had lived too long among the rubble.

Saul asked him, "And who are we supposed to kill?"

The old man started to laugh again as he had when we first entered. "The old woman, you kill her first. She is a sly one. She will tell you that they haven't anything to eat, but she is lying." From his rags the old man drew out a knife. It was old, the kind one uses in the kitchen. Saul took it from the old man's hand and looked at it.

"Why don't you kill her, grandfather?"

This made the old man laugh again, as if the question were a joke. "It is the third house on this side of the street. It looks like a ruin, but they have lots of food." It was hideous: the old man winked as if it now had been his turn to tell a joke.

Saul got up, stuck the knife inside his clothes, and started to move away from the fire.

"Saul," I said.

He turned around and smiled at me; but before I could say any more, he was gone. The old man laughingly began to chant, "He will kill them! He will kill them!"

"Shut up, you demon, or I'll strangle you!" I shouted and held my outstretched fingers up in front of his face.

He ran to a corner of the stable. "Here." I found a stick and gave it to Samuel. "If he comes back to the fire, beat him." I spoke loudly and forcefully. Daniel grabbed my hand. I shoved him away and ran out of the stable to find Saul.

THE OLD PEOPLE | 12

For a moment, when I came outside I could not see, but soon my eyes became accustomed to the darkness. The street was empty. "The third house," I muttered and ran up the street.

"Saul!" I called into the ruin, but no one answered. I climbed over the beam that blocked the entrance and was in the courtyard. It was silent; stories of demons and ghosts filled my mind. "Oh, God," I mumbled. "Oh God, protect me!"

In the doorway of the house, something moved. "Saul?" I whispered breathlessly, believing that it was a ghost.

"Over here," Saul whispered back. I felt a sudden joy as the ghosts disappeared. "Over here."

"Have you . . . Have you killed them?" I whispered as soon as I was near the boy.

He whispered, "Can you smell it?"

I drew the air through my nostrils slowly. Faintly, I could smell roasting meat. Earlier I had forgotten my hunger, but now it came back to me. I kept sniffing as if I were an animal hunting its prey. "Where does it come from?"

Saul pointed beyond the rubble from the roof that was lying in the courtyard. "From over there."

I strained my eyes but I could see nothing.

"Come." Silently as a cat Saul moved across the courtyard. I followed him, but as I was climbing over a pile of rubbish, my foot slipped and a stone fell noisily. I could not see Saul's face, but I am sure that he frowned. In the darker shadows made by one of the still standing walls, we huddled and listened. There was no sound. Saul sniffed.

"Yes," I whispered for now the smell of roasting meat was stronger. A low doorway led to what once must have been the bondsmens' or the servants' quarters. The door was not on its hinges, but it was leaning against the opening. The angle was such that we could enter at one side, by pressing ourselves carefully against the wall. Now we were in total darkness and I wanted to go back.

Trembling, I followed Saul. When he, like a dark

shadow, disappeared inside another doorway, I stood still. I expected that now someone would attack me. I caught up with Saul. The room he had entered was empty. Through a ragged hole in one corner; one could see the stars; otherwise, the roof was intact. Saul picked up two stones from the rubble and handed one to me. It felt strange in my hand and my first impulse was to throw it away; but at the same time, it comforted me and I kept it.

Saul touched my arm and pointed towards a door. Between the door and the casement, there was light. We crept to the door and listened. On the other side of it someone was talking. It was the voice of an old man. He was praying. I could not distinguish the words and yet I thought I understood what he was saying, for I was used to hearing my father pray and since my bar mitzvah I had recited many of the common prayers.

I grabbed Saul's shoulder indicating that I wanted him to wait, to do nothing until the man had finished his prayers. But Saul only glanced back at the doorway through which we had entered the room, to make sure that no one had followed us and that our retreat was secure; then he pushed the door open. I expected it to be locked from the inside, but it was not and opened easily.

The first thing that we saw was the table with a loaf of bread on it, and then the old man who stood beside the table with his prayer shawl over his shoulders. I did not see the old woman before she screamed. She was attending the fire in the corner of the room. She was very fat. The old man paid no attention to us nor to the woman. He kept on reciting his prayers as if we were not there at all.

As fat as the woman was, so thin was the man. His eyes were deep blue and sunken, and his hair was white. I felt that he was throwing the words of the prayer at me as the righteous throw stones at a criminal. 'What he is saying now, he has made up,' I thought, for I had never heard such a prayer.

"Oh God, who has forsaken us, for we have broken the Covenant. Our children are like dogs who fight in the streets over the garbage of other nations. Your words are heard no more in Judea. The mountains that echoed with Your thunder are silent. Your house is burned and plundered, and Your children slaves. God of Abraham and Isaac, Your nation has become like the viper that bites its own young and whose breath is foul from poison. Oh God, who led us out of Egypt, we were not a mighty stream that could flow through the desert without diminishing, we were but a shallow spring which the sand ate." I noticed now that there were tears in the old man's eyes, making them bluer than they were before. I dropped my stone to the floor.

Now that the old man had stopped praying, silence filled the room. "Shalom," I said. "We are hungry."

The woman grabbed the bread from the table and

screamed, "Get out, beggars!" The old man said nothing and she screamed again, "Get out!"

I think it was because she was so fat that I became so enraged. I did not speak to her but to the old man. "In times of war or drought, when the wells are empty, all men are beggars."

The old woman shrieked, "Give them nothing! Tell them to go away!"

"When your brother dies," I said to the old man, "you must take care of your brother's children. Such is the Law."

The old man smiled and said, as if he were talking to himself, "My brother was killed and his children were killed with him."

I glanced at Saul. He was afraid of the old man. I looked at his hand and at once he dropped the stone. The old woman started screaming again, but the old man turned his face towards her and she stopped.

'He belongs to the Sadducees,' I thought. 'He is a man who has owned much and is used to being obeyed when he gives a command.'

"Your brother has died," I began to plead. "So have our fathers and our uncles. Whom shall we turn to? Saul and I have two other children with us. They are in a house not far from here. One of them is so young that he can make a woman smile when she sees him. They are not my brothers; yet they are with me and I want food for them."

The old man turned away; and now he no longer looked like a prophet to me but only an old man. "We have only enough for ourselves," the old woman cried, and bent over the fire to try to hide the meat that was roasting there.

"Give them the meat and the bread you baked yesterday."

The old woman started to wail as if she had been asked to give up her own life. Saul took a rag and laid it out on the table. He took one of the spits out of the fire and with his knife scraped the meat into the piece of cloth. The second spit was smaller than the first and had but ten small pieces of meat on it. The old woman tried to grab it from him.

"Take only half," I ordered. But when the old man smiled approvingly, I shouted at him, "We are four and you are but two. Where is the bread?"

Though she wept, the woman put the bread back on the table. I asked Saul for the knife. I cut the bread in two pieces; the smaller one I left on the table. The old man said nothing; the old woman moaned.

Saul was already at the door. I stood with the bread in one hand and the knife in the other. "May the Lord make you prosper and keep you well." The words seemed stupid and I cursed myself for having said them. Such it is when ordinary words are used in extraordinary situations; they break like sticks that are being asked to perform the work of pillars.

"Shalom," I mumbled. 'Peace,' I thought. But after

the storm when the trees are broken, their roots severed from the earth, what meaning has peace? What comfort has the stillness, after the storm has raged and left all in ruin?

When we returned, the old man was sitting opposite Daniel and Samuel. His eyes gleamed when he saw us. "Did you kill her?" he asked eagerly.

Saul laughed. "We couldn't. She was too fat. You had given me too short a knife, grandfather."

The old man giggled. Suddenly he noticed the bread in my hands and ran towards me. "Give it to me! Give it to me or I shall whip you!"

Saul laughed but I had lost patience with the old man and shoved him away. He fell and began to cry. "I am hungry," he whined.

"Shut up, grandfather," Saul said, "or you'll get nothing."

Obediently he went back to the fire and waited while we shared the meat into five portions. Before dividing the bread I cut it in half, so we would have something for the morning. When the old man had received his portion, he scuttled away to his corner as a dog that feared for his bone. I told the children to eat slowly and when Daniel began to stuff his mouth with food, I took some of his bread away. He didn't cry but just sat and looked up at me. When I gave it back to him, he smiled happily.

I suggested to Saul that we keep watch during the

night, for I did not trust the old man. He agreed and I said that I would sit first and wake him when I grew too sleepy. Daniel and Samuel fell asleep almost at once. Daniel lay as near to me as I would allow him. Saul lay down but could not fall asleep. We talked for a while of what we could do the next day.

The pauses between Saul's words became longer and longer. Finally, just before he fell asleep, he said, "The old man . . . I couldn't have killed him. I would have gone without food sooner than kill him."

I wanted to tell him that I could have killed neither of them, but he was already asleep. 'The old woman,' I thought. 'Saul could have killed her and she was mad. I couldn't have killed either of them. But if I could have, it would have been the old man with his eyes as blue as the sky and his talk of God's revenge upon the Jews.'

I threw some small sticks on the fire. It flared up. The old man returned to the fire. He sat down and stared at me. 'He isn't seeing me,' I thought. His mind was no longer governed by time; what was left of his life would pass as a dream.

'David, who are you?' I asked myself. Then I smiled, for an answer had occurred to me. 'I have come to Jerusalem because I cannot answer that question. When I can, I shall go back to Tyre and become a scholar as my father hopes.'

AMONG THE RUINS | 13

I SLEPT LITTLE that night. I did not wake Saul until just before dawn. During the night, I had decided that I had to find someone to take care of Daniel and Samuel, for I could not do it. As for Saul, although I was not sure that I would not prefer to be alone, I would propose to him that he stay with me. For a long time I sat wondering why, in spite of my doubts, I was preparing arguments to persuade Saul to remain with me. Then I recalled that in Tyre, when I was ten years old, I had had a friend very like Saul.

Noah had been poor. His father could neither read

nor write and he made his living by repairing copper pots and pans. Both my parents had disapproved of my friendship, especially my mother, for Noah was a rude child and would never say thank you for anything he received. Still, for a whole year we had met every day, this being possible because my father would deny me nothing. I had been attracted to Noah, but I had not liked him. Many evenings, I would say to myself, 'Tomorrow, I shall tell him that I don't want to see him again.' Yet when tomorrow came, I would sneak out of the house to find him. Noah had made no secret of the fact that he tolerated my company for what he could gain from it. He pursued charity shamelessly but had none for others. His poor parents he despised, and always referred to his father as "the old beggar."

Why did I want to be in the company of Noah or Saul, I who could not kill a bird and would step out of the way not to crush a worm? . . . To know the difference between good and evil, for this we had lost Paradise. And the Wisdom of God came to me. And I knew surely why we had lost Paradise. And why God need not have sent an angel with a sword of flame to drive us out, for if we knew good and evil we would not want to live in Paradise. Knowledge would have made us always wander away from Paradise, as it had made God dissatisfied with His heaven, so that He had had to create the earth. And I understood — in that cold night, sitting beside the fire, with the head of a child in my lap and an old insane man across from me — what we had gained from eating the apple! Despite the horror of death, despite the cruelty of our knowledge, we had lost Paradise to gain something better. God was angry with Adam and Eve . . . No, that was wrong. God was pleased! He had planted the tree in the Garden so that they would eat of it, and He would become less lonely in His knowledge. We had eaten of the apple to lose Paradise, and had gained knowledge, so that we could conceive of Paradise. My thoughts during that night wandered like pilgrims through the desert; and I felt happy and at peace.

Saul woke me in the morning and showed me where there was a well. There was no copper bucket, only an earthenware pot; and I had to be careful not to smash it against the sides as I lowered it. The water was cool and fresh and I washed myself. I tried to persuade Samuel and Daniel to wash themselves; but they had grown too used to their dirt and refused. Children are not like cats, clean by nature; they have to be forced to wash.

Shortly after I had gone to sleep, Saul had dozed and the old man had tried to steal the bread. Saul had caught him and chased him from the house. I had slept so heavily that I had not heard anything, but Daniel and Samuel had awakened. Now that it was morning, the old man returned and demanded his part of the bread, but Saul would give him nothing. Finally, I gave him half of my portion.

Saul laughed at me. Pointing to Daniel he said, "You could have given that one half your bread. He needs it as much as the old one and that scarecrow — if he had had the strength — would have killed us all last night, for the sake of the bread."

It annoyed me that Saul was right, for I knew that I had given the bread out of weakness, not out of generosity. I was glad when we left the house behind with the old man in it, for I had no wish to see him again.

We walked down to the Lower City. There were more people there. Many had already started repairing their houses. I was looking for a priest or some other leader of the community. Everywhere one saw soldiers but order had returned to the city and the people seemed not to be afraid of them. From two women who had been to a well for water I was told of a man of the Levites whom many sought for advice and help.

The house of Simon ben Judas was hardly damaged and some workmen were repairing the wall and the gates. In the courtyard there were lots of people, many of whom were very poorly dressed and looked hungry as well. In the corner some women were engaged in cooking broth in a large copper caldron.

Titus had killed most of the priests of the Temple, declaring that a nation without a Temple did not need priests. Simon ben Judas was a nephew of one of the priests and the uncle of another, but he himself had always lived as a recluse, caring little for power. Simon ben Judas was wealthy. I had heard my father talk of him. He was the owner of vineyards in the Galilee and around Joppa by the sea. My father had bought wine from him, but had only met his steward. It had annoyed my father, for Simon ben Judas was known as a great scholar.

The anteroom was filled with people waiting to see the master of the house. In one corner four old men were praying. I told Saul to take the children outside, but then decided to keep Daniel with me, for he had a very beautiful and appealing face. I hoped that his countenance would lend weight to my arguments.

Next to the door which led to the rooms of Simon ben Judas stood an elderly servant. His face showed that he knew his own importance and he enjoyed his position. I watched a few people come up to him humbly and be turned away, not always politely.

"I am David ben Joseph. I am from Tyre. I should like to speak to your master." I spoke not in the language of the people but in Hebrew.

The servant answered me in Aramaic, the common language spoken in the Galilee and around Jerusalem. He explained that his master was busy and had given instructions that he was not to be disturbed.

I had guessed correctly. The old servant probably only knew some prayers in Hebrew, but could not speak it. Now I acted as if I had not understood him, and repeated my request, this time in Greek. The servant's face showed irritation and, I thought, a little fear. His Greek, though he understood me, was so poor that all he said was no.

I looked at him a little impatiently and made my request in the language of Rome — of our Latin masters, of that rabble from all corners of the world, that Titus called the Roman army! This the servant did not understand at all, though he guessed which language it was. Once more he repeated in Aramaic that his master would see no one. Indignantly, I spoke once more in Latin. The truth was that I spoke it badly, but then, so did Joseph ben Matthias and most of the other people whom I knew who had not lived in Rome.

Though he continued to frown, the servant left the room, but closed the door behind him so I could not go with him.

He returned hastily and motioned for me to follow him. I glanced at Daniel and decided not to take him with me. The servant led me through a large room which was all but empty of furniture into a smaller one. Seated in a chair, with a blanket around his shoulders and warming his hands over a copper brazier, was Simon ben Judas. I had not expected him to look as he did. I had thought that he would be tall, but he was almost a dwarf.

"My servant said that a Roman spy was waiting outside." Simon ben Judas' voice was not the voice of a dwarf. It was very deep and would have fitted a giant.

"I am not a spy. My name is David ben Joseph. My father is a wine merchant in Tyre. Our caravan was attacked near Mount Carmel and the robbers, who were Samaritans, took me prisoner."

"Mount Carmel?" Simon ben Judas interrupted. "Mount Carmel is far from here."

"The bandits were caught by Roman soldiers and I escaped." I paused, trying to think of some good reason that might explain why I had come to Jerusalem. "I should have gone to Caesarea. We have friends there, Joseph ben Matthias." I gazed appealingly at Simon ben Judas, but he scowled.

"Joseph ben Matthias is an old wineskin which, instead of containing good wine or vinegar, is filled with words; and if you kick him, they gush out in great quantities."

"Or if you pay him," I added.

Simon ben Judas smiled; but then to my confusion, he said, "My hearing is not always good. I thought you said that he was your friend. Not that talking well of their friends is the favorite occupation of the citizens of Jerusalem, but I thought that in Tyre, people behaved differently."

I blushed, not so much for the maliciousness of what I had said as for having been foolish. "Aren't people in all cities alike?" I asked hesitantly.

"I see . . . Since all people are rascals, the most honest are those who admit to their vices." Simon ben

Judas smiled as if he were saying pleasantries; and I could not help thinking that my father had been fortunate in not having met him.

"Forgive me," I said. "Not all cities are alike, nor all people. But Joseph ben Matthias is my father's friend not mine. He was very angry with me when I saw him last."

"Ah, so it was merely then a matter of words and meaning not going hand in hand like good children, but of one staying at home while the other was playing . . . Why was Joseph ben Matthias angry with you?"

I had tried to say what I had thought would please Simon ben Judas. I had failed and I was confused. "What I said to Joseph ben Matthias was that the Masada would not fall as Jotapata had."

Simon ben Judas laughed. "Yes, that would have enraged him . . . I believe that no act he will ever do for the rest of his life will not in some way be a defense of why he did not defend Jotapata . . . So in Caesarea they have heard that the Masada is still held by the Zealots."

"Yes," I answered. "The people in the streets — the poor and the young — speak of it; but the old people say that nothing will come of it."

Simon ben Judas, who was neither young nor old, smiled. "The old people are right. Nothing will come of it. The Zealots will be killed and forgotten."

"Everyone knows about the Greek wars of hundreds

of years ago. They know of the war against Troy."

This time my words made him laugh boisterously, but he looked at me kindly.

"Hector was killed," I continued, "but every Greek and Roman knows his name."

Simon ben Judas stopped laughing and said, "I wonder if that fact made his pain less when he died . . . If you are a poet, go to the Masada." He looked away from me and stared into the brazier. "No, go to Rome. Blind yourself there with your own importance. And then write about the brave defenders: about their heroic speeches and their courageous death."

I had not understood him and Simon ben Judas could read my dismay in my face. Gently, he said, "Your father has educated you well. Do you know the Torah and the history of Our People?" I nodded and Simon ben Judas asked, "Who is your hero of the Trojan War?"

"Hector!" I exclaimed as if the question could only be answered thus.

Again Simon ben Judas laughed. This time until tears ran down his face. "A man might answer otherwise and have a brain, but not a heart." He dried his eyes. "But you are wrong in one thing: not every Roman or Greek knows the story of Troy, any more than every citizen of Jerusalem knows the Torah. Now tell me: Who is your hero in our history?"

First I thought of David, then of Solomon; but neither of them was a hero to me. I thought of Judas

Maccabeus, but even about him there were things that I did not admire. Abraham . . . Moses . . . They weren't heroes either. In my bewilderment, I said, "I don't know."

Simon ben Judas looked at me intently and then, lowering his voice, as if he were about to tell me a secret, he said, "Now you know the glory of the Torah and our histories. There are no Jewish heroes. All were men, subject to the weakness of the flesh: Children of Adam, every one. That is why, when the Greeks will tire you, like too much wine, you will return to the Torah, and it will be to you as the springs of Ein-Gedi are to a man who has wandered in the desert."

His words made me quiver and I felt happy. "Joseph ben Matthias says that God has left the Jews, that they are no longer His People."

Simon ben Judas pursed his lips, shrugged his shoulders, and turned away, as one does when a child has said something ridiculous. "Joseph ben Matthias' idea of God is himself, enlarged out of all proportion. He thinks himself a scholar and a general, but he is neither. He would never hold with a man who loses, so he thinks that God wouldn't either. His God of the Jews is a circumcised Zeus." His final words must have pleased Simon ben Judas, for he repeated them and laughed. He stopped laughing abruptly, "You must have come here for some reason."

I told him about the children, Daniel and Samuel; how I had met them when they were going to turn bandits in Samaria. I told him about Joseph and Saul, too.

"We are collecting the children who have no parents. We shall feed them as best we can, but there are many. Take Daniel and Samuel to the woman in the courtyard whose name is Sarah . . . She is a match for any Abraham, but she has a good heart. She will take care of them. But what about yourself? Do you want me to help you to return to Tyre?"

"I don't know what I want," I admitted.

"Here." He took from a leather purse three silver coins. "Take these. You can sleep in the stable, it is warm there. I am probably the only Jew in Jerusalem who still has donkeys and horses. Come tomorrow, at the same time, and tell me what you have decided to do and in what ways I can help you."

'What a strange man Simon ben Judas is,' I thought. 'What other man as old as my father would have listened to a fifteen-year-old and asked him what he wanted to do?' I thanked Simon ben Judas and left the room. At the door, I bowed. When I raised my head, I looked at him again. He was staring into the embers of the brazier. As I closed the door as silently as I could, I thought, 'I was wrong. My father need not have feared meeting Simon ben Judas. He would have been kind to him.'

OUTSIDE THE WALLS | 14

I STAYED ALL WINTER with Simon ben Judas and did not leave Jerusalem before the spring flowers had wizened on the hills around the city. I called him Rabbi Simon because he had agreed to be my master. He was a good teacher for he had patience and praised understanding more than knowledge. Knowledge is the tools needed for work, but without understanding it is as useless as the carpenter's tools are to a man without arms.

I had not decided when I left Simon ben Judas' room to stay in his house in Jerusalem — this thought had not even occurred to me. From his room, I went directly to the courtyard to look for the woman called Sarah. She was middle-aged and listened patiently when I explained that Simon ben Judas had suggested that she take care of Daniel and Samuel. She was not the kind of woman who got tears in her eyes when she saw a beautiful baby. Her lips were thin and she seldom smiled. Her duty — as she conceived it — was sacred to her and she worked very hard. She was a person that it was easier to honor and respect than to love; but now, when feeding the starving children was more important than loving them, she saved hundreds from death.

Daniel was frightened when I presented the two boys to her. He cried and clung to me. I felt sorry for him, yet I forced him to take the hand of the young woman whom Sarah had called to take both him and Samuel to the house not far away which had been made into a dwelling place for orphans. I watched them walk through the courtyard and out of the gate. I wondered if I had, until now, realized how small they were.

"It's good we got rid of them."

I had almost forgotten Saul. As his words echoed my own feelings, I turned angrily and said, "I would have kept them with me if I could have."

Saul smiled knowingly and I looked away. "Come," I said gruffly, "I'll show you the stable where Simon ben Judas says we can sleep."

Before we reached the door of the stable we could hear the hum of many people talking. As I had been warned, the animals were still there. Old people sat in groups and talked in low voices to each other. In one corner I saw a young woman with a baby in her arms, and I thought, 'I hope she has milk, so that it does not cry tonight.'

We returned to the courtyard. The soup wasn't ready yet, and I said to Saul that we would not wait. Now that I had money, I felt doubly hungry.

It was noon. Near the gates of the city we found a stall where lamb was being roasted. But first we must buy a bread, for I could not afford that we satisfy our hunger on meat alone. I broke the bread exactly in half and gave one piece to Saul. It gave me a strange kind of pleasure to know that if Saul had received the three silver coins, he would have given me nothing. I cannot tell whether that lamb was well roasted and contained the proper spices, for hunger improves the worst cooking. Even after I was full, I was tempted to buy more meat, for those who have starved cannot be really satisfied. They look upon food as a miser does upon coins; and sometimes a man who has starved long will steal food from his own table when he has plenty, to hide it in the room where he sleeps.

Near the stall a young man was sitting on the ground playing the eight-stringed harp and singing. At first I did not notice him. His voice was thin and he sang badly. He kept his head bowed, so that his words could be heard only when one stood next to him and listened intently:

"Oh Daughters of Judea,
You have shed too many tears,
What song of tomorrow
Can bring comfort to your ears?
The strings of the harp
Are tuned by sorrow's hand.
Mount Zion's back is bare
And death is over the land."

Few people stopped to hear him, which was not only because he could not sing well. Before the siege a singer, even a poor one, could attract listeners; but now people were ashamed to stop when they could give nothing. I bent down and held out two copper coins, which was enough to buy a bread; but the singer continued his verse. I stepped back, and as I did so he lifted his head: he was blind. I put the coins into his hand and he blessed me.

It was one of those clear days that usually come in winter, especially in Jerusalem; all the objects in the distance appear very near, as if a line has been drawn around each to make sure it is noticed. "In Jerusalem, the sky has disappeared, so that the prayers and offerings of the people can better pass up to God." This explanation was given to me by a man in Tyre, who had been born in Jerusalem.

We walked beyond the walls, which the Romans had started to demolish, past Herod's Wall, to one of the camps of the Romans. No one bothered us or asked us why we had come. There were many other children about, some were trying to get work from the Romans, so they could earn their bread. There were also men selling wares to the soldiers. During the day strangers were allowed in the Roman camps, but as soon as the sun set the guards turned everyone away and it could cost a man his life to be found there without a permit.

Saul knew many of the boys we met. He stopped them to ask the news. We were told that troops had been sent to Herod's Tomb and to Machærus. Both places were defended by the People of the Law. Machærus was beyond the Sea of Salt, but Herodium was less than a day's march from Jerusalem. The troops had been made eager for the attack by being told that Herod's Tomb was made of gold. They were commanded by a Roman named Lucilius Bassus, who was known for his cruelty.

Once a group of officers approached us from behind. They were preceded by eight soldiers who ordered us roughly to get out of the way. One of the officers had a gold breast plate and we were told that he was Flavius Silva.

In the late afternoon we left the Roman camp. I bought another bread, which I shared with Saul. We walked slowly while we ate it; and I tried to think about what I would do, where I would go. My thoughts were like the pebbles that one picks up on the beach without purpose and throws away without notice. I did not know what I wanted to do.

"Judas Maccabeus kept the Law and so did Jonathan!" Someone was shouting loudly and angrily. We were just outside the city gate. A young man with unkempt hair and beard and clothes that revealed his poverty was standing on a heap of rubble. A small crowd had gathered in front of him. "And God was pleased! Above Simon, too, God held his hand. But John forgot the ways of his father and gave power to those who read what should not be read, to those who know what should not be known."

We were on the fringe of the crowd now. "They speak of the Law and claim to care about the Torah; but to them the words of the Prophets are like the winds. They copy the Greeks and read the works of the gentiles!"

I was about to walk on; but to my surprise, Saul was listening. "They drink from golden goblets and offer to foreign gods. They say that they are sons of Zadoc, David's priest, who descended from Aaron; but I say they are sons of Rome, sons of those who worship the Golden Calf!" The speaker was talking of the Sadducees. He made a long list of their supposed crimes and blamed them for the loss of the war. His audience was friendly and many grunted or shouted in agreement, especially when he spoke of the wealth of the Sadducees.

My father considered himself a Pharisee and so did Joseph ben Matthias, though he was by birth a Sadducee. Many of the accusations against the Sadducees were true. They accepted only the Torah as Law; and thought nothing of the rabbis and the sages and their interpretations. Many of them were rich. Most of the priests belonged to their party. But the Sadducees were not the cause of our defeat; to say this was stupid, for we had fought against the might of Rome, which had defeated more powerful nations than ours. Besides, dissension had weakened us; and for this not only the disagreements between the Sadducees and the Pharisees had been responsible, but even more costly had been the arguments among the Pharisees themselves, for they formed the much larger party.

But to find a single reason for a disaster will always be popular — and the braying of a donkey in Jerusalem sometimes is heard in Joppa. I wanted to go on, for I feared that I should become angry and get into a discussion with the young man, which I knew would gain me nothing.

Saul would not leave. "He's a fool," I whispered to him. He pretended that he had not heard me. "I am going," I said a little louder. He shrugged his shoulders, and did not even turn his head when I walked away. By now there was a crowd of at least fifty people.

I climbed to the ruins of the Temple. The sun had set but the tops of the mountains looked as if they had been painted in blood.

I was alone. "Who am I?" I whispered; and then listened as if I expected an answer. A rat ran out from under a pile of stones. It stood still, sniffed the cold evening air, and then disappeared.

"Oh, God of Judas Maccabeus, were You the God of Solomon as well? Please, God, who led us out of Egypt, lead me out of my own thoughts!" The words brought me no comfort and tears came into my eyes.

"I am alone, God! I am alone!" I shouted but the night around me was silent.

IT WAS DARK when I returned to Simon ben Judas' house and the entrance gate was locked. I called and the same old man who had led me to his master's room that afternoon answered from behind the barred door, "This door is locked at sunset. If your heart is pure then return in the morning and my master will speak with you."

I was not sure whether the servant knew who I was, so I begged him to forgive me for the different languages I had spoken to him to gain entrance to Simon ben Judas. Probably because he remembered how long his master had talked with me, he then unbarred the gate.

Once inside, I thanked him and we spoke together in Aramaic for he, like my father, was from the Galilee and spoke this language well. He told me that twice robbers had tried to break down the gates, and that on the same street, a whole family had been murdered the week before. "What times we live in," he muttered.

I was at the point of asking him whether Simon ben Judas was a Sadducee; but I feared that he would ask me why I wanted to know, and my reply would augment his anxiety. 'In any case, would it matter?' I asked myself silently. 'To the young orator I had heard, Simon ben Judas would be a Sadducee, as would my father, for they were rich.' But as my indignation against the young man rose to fury, I felt a sudden shame: For what had I been praying if not for an answer to all questions? I had wanted God to point out whom I could hate and whom I should love. I bid the old man good night. Walking towards the stable, I felt at peace; and that is God's blessing.

The stable was not completely dark. An oil lamp burned in a niche in the wall. When my eyes had accustomed themselves to the twilight, I could see well enough not to step on any of the sleeping people. How many we were, I did not count; but it took me a few minutes to find a place to lie down. I found one, finally, beside a wall. The air in the stable was warm, but the earthen floor was cold. I fumbled my way to where I had noticed there was some hay and took an armful of it.

I dreamt I was at home in Tyre. I was again a little boy. We were sitting down to supper; my father was saying the prayer when someone knocked on our door. My father stopped praying and the room was silent; but the knocking on the door continued. Then I awoke, but for a moment I thought I was still in the dream. Someone who stumbled over my feet cursed me and I sat up. Everyone was awake.

Out in the courtyard, I saw Simon ben Judas standing next to the old servant. The moon was up and I could see his features plainly. From beyond the wall, I heard the rumble of many feet and shouting. They were trying to break down the door. The door was heavy and barred by a great beam; but each time they struck it, it seemed to give way a little.

"Who are they?" I asked an old man standing near me. A piece of straw was hanging from his beard.

"God has turned against His People," he answered and turned away from me; then he began to mumble what I took to be a prayer.

I ran to the gate to look at the doors. They would hold for a while yet. Fortunately, the street was not broad and the beam they were using was short. Above the roar, I heard someone scream, "Greek! Greek!"

As I made my way to Simon ben Judas, a stone flew

past me. I ducked, though it would not have hit me. "What do they want?" I asked.

"Whatever can be found here . . . And more than that, they want revenge on the Romans. They want to punish someone for what has happened to them."

Now there were several voices screaming, "Greek! Greek!"

"If you seek the Greeks," I shouted as loud as I could. "Then they are camped outside the city. Follow your hearts and when they beat with fear, then you are near them!"

A volley of stones answered me. I bent down, picked up a stone, and threw it back over the wall. Many other people in the courtyard followed my example.

"No!" shouted Simon ben Judas. "Too many stones have been thrown by Jews against other Jews. From my house no stones shall be thrown."

Such was the power of Simon ben Judas, that no one again dared to pick up a stone and throw it. When he saw that we would obey him, he told us in his deep voice a story. While he spoke we paid no attention to the noises from the other side of the wall and as little as possible to the stones that were cast into the courtyard.

"At the time — not long ago — when Aristobulus and his brother, Hyrcanus, were fighting over Judea, like two dogs over a bone, there lived a wise man, whose name was Onias. When Aristobulus had fled with his men to the Temple, Hyrcanus besieged the Temple. Hyrcanus, who until now had been thought to be the victor, became angry when the Temple held. He asked Onias to pray to God to destroy Aristobulus and his men. With his face towards the Temple, Onias prayed thus: 'Oh God, the King of the Whole World, since those who stand with me, outside the wall, are Your People, and those who are besieged are also Thy Priests, I beseech Thee, that Thou wilt hearken neither to the prayers of these against those, nor bring to affect what those pray against these.' . . . Let us be like that wise man and not answer a brother's stone with a stone."

Just as Simon ben Judas finished speaking a stone hit his shoulder and he fell to the ground. His servant helped him up. His face was disfigured by pain. He was carried inside the house and several of the older people followed him.

I had not noticed it — for the shouting and the stone throwing continued — but the people who had been trying to break down the door had stopped. The dull boom . . . boom of the beam as it hit the door had ceased. 'Maybe they have given up,' I thought. I stood completely still; now I could smell the wood burning. I knew what they were preparing to do. They had built a fire against the door and were hoping to burn it down.

"Water!" I shouted and turned towards the stable door, where a group of women stood. "Get the pots from the kitchen."

I ran to the well and let down the bucket. When I drew it up, I realized that in my haste I had spilled half of the water.

Potful after potful of water was thrown under the portals, so that it would seep out on the street and put out their fire. As soon as the people outside understood our purpose, they doubled their stone throwing and several people were hurt. We could hear that they were having trouble with the fire; then I heard someone call for straw.

When the first of the burning fagots came over the wall, it landed in the courtyard and a bucket of water put it out. But the second hit the roof of one of the lower buildings, where grain and wool were stored. Someone climbed up to get it and throw it down into the yard. A stone hit the man and screaming he fell from the roof. When he hit the ground, he was silent.

His eyes were closed but he was still breathing. When one of the other men touched him, he moaned. The scream of the man had been greeted by a shout of joy from the men in the street. As I helped carry the wounded man into the stable, I thought, 'They will kill us all!'

The smell of smoke grew stronger, but it was not from our house. Up the street, the crowd had attacked another building, which they had managed to set afire. Some of those who had stood before our house must have left, for fewer stones were being cast over the wall. Two more burning fagots came, but they landed harmlessly in the courtyard, where they were trampled out.

Suddenly there seemed to be less noise and then came the shout: "Soldiers! Soldiers!"

We heard the sound of the Roman soldiers, entering from both ends of the street. The people were caught between the two groups of marching men; and now their screams were desperate.

"Brothers," a voice cried. "Let us in or they will kill us!" And the tone of the voice told the truth of the message.

I ran to the entrance and tried to remove the beam that locked the doors. The old man who had said that God had given up His People held onto my arms. "They will kill us, too."

I knew he was right, but still I tried to open the doors. Several men came to help the old one and I was dragged away.

The screams in the street told of the slaughter on the other side of the wall. I put my hands up to my ears not to hear; but my hands could not protect me and I fled to the stable.

I closed the door behind me. The smell and warmth of the animals met me and comforted me. I leaned my head against the wall and closed my eyes. Not far from me someone was mumbling a prayer. A song was being sung to make a child sleep. I listened and slowly I understood the words, for I knew the song:

"The Lord, will I at all times bless,
With praise my voice will sing.
My soul shall in Jehovah boast
The meek shall hear with joy.

"Oh, let us magnify the Lord
Exalt His name with me.
I sought the Lord, and he me heard
And from all fears set me free."

Suddenly I started to laugh loudly; I had remembered something. The woman stopped singing and the baby started to cry. In an angry voice, she asked me why I was laughing. I was laughing too hard, I could not tell her. I laughed until I cried. I let myself slide down the wall till I lay on the floor.

I had remembered the fate of Onias: When he had finished the prayer — the one Simon ben Judas told us about — he had been stoned to death!

SIMON BEN JUDAS | 16

NOT BEFORE the sun rose did we dare open the gate, for we feared the soldiers as much as we did the mob. Outside in the street we found thirty bodies. Not one among the dead had not been poor and many were so thin that one might have supposed they had died of starvation. Among them I recognized the young man whom I had heard speak the day before. I looked for the body of Saul; but either he had not been among the rioters or he had escaped.

The house up the street which had been looted and set on fire was now only a ruin, in which smoke still smoldered. Also there were dead bodies there. Of the family who had lived in that house, only a small child survived. Four other houses had been broken into, but the inhabitants had not been harmed.

Simon ben Judas had all the bodies carried into the courtyard of his house. Prayers were said and they were carried to the graveyard. They were all buried before sunset as it has been decreed. But who was there to weep over their deaths? Sorrow multiplied beyond understanding does not increase. Tears cannot cleanse the eyes of those who have seen too much. Sorrow softens the heart; but horror and cruelty harden it, until it is only a fit dwelling place for hate.

That afternoon we learned that the Romans had taken prisoners and they were to suffer a worse fate than those who had been killed: They were to be crucified.

I went to see the condemned as they were being led to their deaths. I looked at each man's face, searching for Saul. I realized with horror that many did not yet understand their fate. Two of the condemned were only boys, twelve or thirteen years old. I did not see Saul and I asked the Roman soldier whether there were others who had been taken prisoner. He shook his head. He was an old man and though he probably had helped to crucify many prisoners, his face was pale with knowledge of his duty.

When I returned to the house, I asked to see Simon ben Judas; and I was led to the same room where he had talked to me the day before. It seemed to me that in that short time since our last conversation he had aged. His voice broke several times; and once or twice he whispered so that I had to listen intently. He had not been seriously hurt, but his back ached and he moved his left arm with difficulty. He asked me whether I knew what had happened to those who had been taken prisoner. I told him that they were on their way to their deaths; they had been condemned in the morning.

"Roman Law runs so fast that it leaves justice behind . . . Are they to be crucified?"

I nodded.

"This Roman method of putting criminals to death fills me with revulsion! Many people have lived so long on the cross that they have died of thirst and hunger. The Romans call all but the Greeks barbarians, yet cruelty is the shadow that walks beside the Roman legions. We Jews, according to God's Law, put to death our criminals by stoning . . . I have no wish for anyone's death and would not throw a stone at a defenseless man, but our Law is more just. For those who judge must also throw the stones; they cannot escape the cloak of responsibility . . . The Roman officer, between two gulps of wine, says the word 'guilty'; or turns his thumbs down while one of his hands grasps the leg of a chicken. He does not know what the word means, for he is listening to a poet playing on a harp. While he reclines on a couch, the word 'guilty' becomes a screaming man, a world of pain nailed to the cross.

That same officer may shudder when he rides past the bird-eaten corpse; he will not remember whose word it was that made carrion of a living man."

I waited but Simon ben Judas said no more. "My friend Saul was not among them . . . I wish they all had escaped!"

"Had they broken down the doors last night, they would have killed us . . ." He bowed his head. "Though I, too, wish they had escaped. It is a terrible death," he whispered. His lips parted. Again he appeared as if he were about to continue, but he said nothing, though I waited long.

"Why . . . Why would they have killed us?"

Simon ben Judas smiled sadly. "Because of the gate being barred, for one good reason."

I thought he was dismissing my question but I persisted, "Why because the door was barred?"

Simon ben Judas thought for a while before he answered. "When the Children of Israel traveled through the other lands and had no home, the guarding of the Ark of the Covenant was of the greatest importance; and all the rituals were observed. Once we were settled and the Temple stood in Jerusalem, we had less use for the Ark. It was a symbol, as the standard of a Roman legion is a symbol of home and of the power of Rome to the soldiers."

I was angry. How could Simon ben Judas talk of the Holy Ark and the standards of the Roman legions

— the Roman butchers! — in the same breath? 'Maybe they were right about him,' I thought, 'when they screamed "Greek!" '

"We have many symbols," he continued. "Most of them we do not even think about. A barred gate is a symbol, too. The people in the street, last night, were hungry. The night was cold. When they came up the street, they thought of plunder; when they found a barred door, they thought of murder."

"Why did they shout, 'Greek'?" I asked.

Simon ben Judas shrugged his shoulders. The movement brought him pain and he grimaced. "Symbols we cannot do without or all poets would be mute. But symbols are also dangerous. Think of fire: it can warm you but it may also burn down your house. 'Greek' is a word of hate, a symbol of our defeat; and it is thrown like a stone."

'This is not a real answer,' I thought with annoyance. "Yesterday I heard a young man say," I said aloud, "that it was a sin to read in the Greek language; and that our defeat was caused by our priests, with whom God was angry, because they studied the works of the gentiles instead of His Law."

"It is true," he began softly, "that many who belonged to the priesthood and called themselves Sadducees were blinded by pride in their worldly position. They felt that the Law was enough and that being the protectors of the Law gave them the right to censure the sages. But as to the reading of Greek texts . . ." Simon ben Judas smiled. "Most of them were too lazy to read even in Hebrew. If they cared about imitating the Greeks and the Romans, it was not their scholars they had in mind, but their choice of food and dancing girls that attracted them . . . But this was not true of all the Sadducees —," and here his voice grew sharp, "— any more than it would be fair to say of the Pharisees that all of them felt so *perushim* — so saintly, so chosen — that they could not understand that God had made the Covenant with all the Children of Israel, and not with them alone (for they consider only themselves worthy). Yet it is true that many of them in their study of the Torah and the sages felt superior to the prophets whose words they were interpreting. I can remember a discussion between two Pharisees — equal in ignorance — which ended with their spitting at each other like boys in the streets. They had been arguing over the meaning of a word which neither of them understood."

Simon ben Judas had himself become so furious that I smiled. He noticed it, and he began to laugh so freely that he coughed and almost choked with laughter. "Oh, David . . . Men are like donkeys: they love to bray!"

At that moment I knew that I wanted to stay with him, for only a man who can laugh at himself is worth following. This I said to Simon ben Judas.

"I do not want followers. I am not a holy man or a scholar," he said seriously.

I pleaded that because of my ignorance I would not notice his lack of learning.

Simon ben Judas narrowed his eyes and said, "And because you are not very holy, you will not mind when I break the Laws?"

Simon ben Judas' mood had changed. "To be holy," I said hesitantly, "is a gift that God gave to the Prophets; one cannot search for it . . . The gods of the Romans did not choose them; therefore, they must bribe their gods. Being chosen left us choiceless; and therefore, we cannot put the gods of the gentiles in our Temple . . ." I stopped; words came but they did not express my thoughts. "I know the Laws and keep them . . . I have read the Torah over and over . . . And I am still confused."

Simon ben Judas said sardonically, "Maybe that is why God has chosen us . . . Of all the nations on earth, we looked the most confused." Turning from me, he added, "You will have to sleep in the stable."

RACHEL | 17

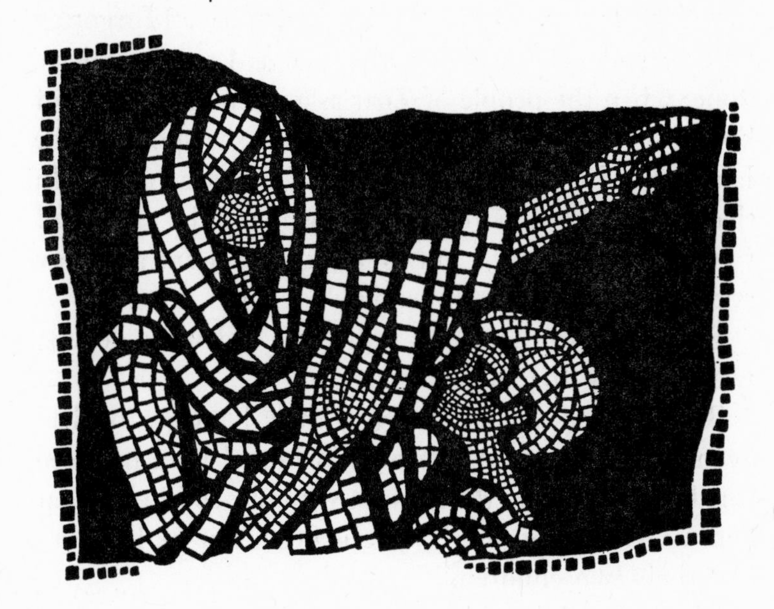

"AND WHAT do you want of me?" This was the usual way that Simon ben Judas started his interview with those who had come to seek his aid. For more than a week, I had been the guardian of his door and I was used to the ways of my master. He usually spoke roughly, but turned few people away without some kind of help, if only a few copper coins. The woman to whom he was now speaking had been waiting to see him since dawn, and she looked as if she had come from far. "Are you dumb, or have you forgotten how to talk?"

The woman glanced at her hands, which she held in

front of her. "No, I am not dumb, nor have I forgotten speech; and yet I search for words as Lot might have done, when the people of Zoar asked him of the fate of Sodom." Her voice was pleasant and she spoke in the language of the Torah. "I come from Machærus. In that city I was the wife of a merchant and the mother of two children. Now I am in Jerusalem. I am a widow and am the mother of no one."

Rabbi Simon ben Judas sighed. "And what do you want, money for food?"

The woman shook her head as if his question had been meaningless. "My brother whom I have not seen for three years is on the Masada with my cousin, Eleazar ben Ya'ir. My brother's wife is dead, but he has with him their two children."

I looked at her with more curiosity than was polite, for she was the cousin of Eleazar ben Ya'ir, the commander of the Masada, whose name was well known even in the streets of Joppa and Caesarea. I glanced at Rabbi Simon, trying to guess his thoughts.

"I want the children," the woman said firmly as if it were in the power of Simon ben Judas to give them to her.

"How should I be able to help you?"

The woman glanced at me; then she whispered, "I have been told that you can send a message there."

"I have been told . . ." Simon ben Judas interrupted himself; he had been about to say something sarcastic. He smiled as one does when one is resigned and annoyed at being so. He had many strange visitors, men who had traveled far to see him; and I was always sent out of the room when he spoke with them. Yet I knew, too, that his contacts with places far from Jerusalem were reliable and many. After he had agreed to let me be his follower, Rabbi Simon had asked me to write a message to my father and to give it to him; in shorter time than it took the full moon to wane, I held in my hands a letter from my father.

"And why do you want the children?" Rabbi Simon asked.

"Even if I had not lost my own children, I would have wanted them; but now I think of them day and night. When the Romans take the Masada, they will kill all the men and sell the women and children into slavery."

"But what if those on the Masada," Rabbi Simon argued, "leave that piece of Herod's vanity, and let General Silva have it without his even having to bother to leave Jerusalem?"

Bitterly the woman said, "If you believe in such a plan, then you do not know my cousin. When he was a child he complained that he was not born in a more heroic time. In one day, he was Saul, David, Joshua, and Judas Maccabeus. Eleazar will not give up the Masada. Though you say it was built by Herod's vanity, it fits the vanity of Eleazar ben Ya'ir."

"What is your name?" Rabbi Simon asked.

"Rachel," she replied.

"I should have thought Leah more fitting for she had the deep pride, while Rachel's was shallow." Smiling, he turned to me, "Beware of studying our history so closely, David, that you forget that it is the past. We can only learn from it if we remember that the ways of God are never repeated."

"My cousin," Rachel said, "lives only in himself. If he ordered the sun to stand still, it would be daylight for him, though it was night for everyone else."

"I promise you nothing. If I should hear of someone traveling to the Masada, I shall have him carry a message there. Since you have no relatives in Jerusalem, you can stay here. You can work in the house where the children live who have no parents."

Rachel turned and I thought she was going to leave, but she kneeled in front of Simon ben Judas and said, "I shall obey you as if you were my father." Rabbi Simon blessed her and I opened the door to let her out.

"David," he said as soon as the door was closed. "I have often thought of a very vexing problem: Who ate the most apples? Eve ate first, '*She took of the tree,*' it says. But we don't know how many apples she had eaten before she gave some to Adam. Suppose that she ate five and he ate only three. Or was it the other way around? My brother had a wife who made me think that Eve had only just nibbled on one. But this woman — Rachel — makes me think that Eve had a healthy appetite."

Simon ben Judas looked very serious but I was not afraid to laugh, for he often looked serious when he was telling a joke and smiled mockingly when he mentioned something about which he cared very much. Yet in the midst of my laughter I was reminded again that he had been called a Greek.

"Are there any more?" Rabbi Simon gestured towards the door. "I am a little tired, David. Distribute money, enough for a meal, if that is what they came for, and bid them come back in the morning."

In the anteroom, I opened the purse Rabbi Simon had given me and gave a few copper coins to each of the people waiting to see him. One young man, however, refused the alms and demanded to see Simon ben Judas at once. He was the most poorly dressed of all those present, and yet he carried himself as if he were used to giving commands. "Tell him that Joab is here," he said in a low tone and I did not dare argue with him.

To Rabbi Simon I apologized, "He acts as if he were carrying a spear and had a sword at his side."

"Let him in," he said with a sigh. "I will speak with him alone." As I was about to open the door my master stopped me, "Find out, David, what the name of Rachel's brother is, and also the names of his children."

I held the door open and the man who called himself Joab walked past me without a nod.

I found Rachel talking with two other women in that part of the courtyard where the cooking fires burned.

She had been given bread, and certainly she must have been hungry, but she did not gulp her food. She was a woman between twenty-five and thirty years old. I do not think that she was beautiful by the standards of the marketplace. There the best earthen pot, or copper pitcher, is the one that looks most like all the others, and has to recommend it that it has no blemishes. Rachel resembled no other woman. Maybe it was the way she walked, the way she held her head, that proclaimed that she could be compared only to herself.

I explained my errand and she told me the names. "Was he from the Masada?" I knew she was referring to Joab, but I merely shrugged my shoulders. "He looked like one of them. He came from the desert."

"Oh, I think you are right," I admitted.

We had walked away from the other women and were standing in the center of the courtyard. "Your cousin . . . Eleazar ben Ya'ir . . ." And then because I did not know how to phrase what I wanted to ask I said foolishly, "Do you like him?"

The woman repeated my words as if they were meaningless sounds, and then she exclaimed to my astonishment, "I hate him!" She turned away from me and walked back to the other women.

SLOWLY DURING the winter the city changed. Houses were repaired and many people who had fled returned. Again one might hear a young woman sing as she carried water back from the well. The marketplace in the Lower City was opened and there was food for sale in the stalls. But it was only on the surface that the wounds were healing; in any of the ruins you might find sick and starving people, who waited not for spring but for death. The strongholds of Jewish resistance had fallen one after the other: first Herodium and then Machærus. Only the fortress of the Masada was still unconquered by the

Romans; but we all knew that it, too, would fall. The dreams of the Maccabees seemed now as unreal as stories told to children. Judea was a province of Rome and the sons of Israel had lost their land.

I often spoke with Rachel of the defenders of the Masada. They grew in my mind until they were giants, whose shadows reached Jerusalem. But Rachel sometimes spoke of them with hatred. She worshipped Simon ben Judas. Once I pointed out to her that he was almost a dwarf and that I had heard that he had a blemish on his body so that he could not enter the Temple. She grew so angry that she forgot herself and hit me. No one saw her do it, and therefore, I could forgive her; but for a whole week we did not speak together. It was she who approached me so that we became friends again.

I no longer slept in the stable but in the room which Simon ben Judas used to receive his guests. She came to me there. It was evening and Rabbi Simon had gone to bed. I was reading by the poor light of a very small oil lamp. I was very much surprised when the door opened and Rachel entered, for she lived in another part of the house where the women's rooms were.

"What are you reading?" she asked boldly.

I looked down at the scroll, which I had let roll itself together at the sound of Rachel's entrance. "The first of the Songs . . . But it is very poorly copied and there are many mistakes." I started to unroll the scroll. "The scribe has forgotten two words. It should say, '*Oh, how long should it be that Thou will hide Thy face from me.*' But the scribe has forgotten to write '*Thy face,*' so the line reads, '*will hide from me.*'

Softly Rachel read aloud the whole of the Song; and I was amazed that she, a woman, could read.

"I am sorry I was so angry with you the other day."

I rolled up the scroll and said, "It does not matter. I was wrong in speaking of Rabbi Simon in the manner I did." The silence between us then grew so long that I had to break it. "It was the way you spoke of them . . . You know that they will all die."

"You don't understand," she replied.

I frowned, for I did not like being told that there was something that I did not understand.

"You admire them because you do not know them."

'You hate them because you think that you know them,' I thought, but I said nothing.

"Are we friends?" she asked gently. I nodded but did not say anything. As she opened the door, I looked up at her and she said, " 'Oh, how long will it be that thou will hide from me?' " She smiled and closed the door behind her.

I remember well the day that the messengers came from the Masada. It was the day after Rabbi Simon had presented me with a scroll from the histories, wherein was written the story of King Saul. It was a very fine copy, rolled on a carved ebony stick. Now that the Temple with its Room of Books had been destroyed, Rabbi Simon had the largest library in Jerusalem.

There were two men: Joab, who had come from the Masada before, and a man whom I later learned was called Simon the Essene, for he belonged to that sect of our people. Simon was tall and thin, and his facial expression was very severe. I took an immediate dislike to him, although he was more polite to me than Joab was. What they said to Simon ben Judas I do not know, for I was not allowed to remain in the room during their conversation with him. The message they brought from the Masada for Rachel could not have been the one that she had hoped for. Rabbi Simon was angry, and though he gave them money, it was not a large amount. As soon as they had departed, he ordered me to fetch Rachel.

As I was leaving his room, he said, "David, I would give up the Masada for the life of a single child."

For the first time it occurred to me — for I had not thought about it before — that Rabbi Simon had no children. As I walked to the house of the orphans, I wondered at the meaning of his words. So many children had died in Jerusalem and all the other cities of Judea: A child's life had no value at all.

Rachel was washing clothes. As soon as she saw me, she knew I had come for her; and when I said that Rabbi Simon wished to talk with her, she guessed the reason. "So they didn't bring them!"

I knew she meant the children and I wanted to tell

her that I was sorry, but I had no words to express it. I didn't understand her longing: How could I have? I was a boy of fifteen and she was a grown woman who had had children of her own. More than once she had spoken of her children. The girl — she had been the oldest — had been six when the soldiers killed her. After he had killed her children, Rachel had begged the soldier to kill her as well; but the sight of a woman on her knees begging him to murder her had made him flee from the house.

Rachel herself had dug the graves of her children. Her husband had been killed in the defense of the city; and to all those who had died with arms in their hands, the Roman commander had denied burial. Even the most barbarian people care for the bodies of their dead, and the Roman knew that the God of Israel had written in the Law how we must bury ours. Oh, how can one tell of these things, except in words like these? Sorrow and joy fit the harp; but what lies beyond grief must be told in plain words that can be cut in stone, not written on parchment.

"I have a message for you from your cousin." Rabbi Simon paused.

"No word from my brother?" Rachel asked.

Rabbi Simon shook his head.

"He won't let the children go," she said and looked at the floor.

"Eleazar ben Ya'ir sent me this message: 'If you dam

up water to make a lake, you must make sure that the dam is strong, for if but a trickle of water escapes, the lake will follow . . . Therefore, no one must leave the Masada.' "

Rachel, as she spoke, looked at Simon ben Judas; but I think she was seeing Eleazar ben Ya'ir. "And you dam up water to give life to the crops when the summer sun burns them; but in the mountains, near the Lake of Asphalt, there are no crops to drink the water and gain life. There is only sand to drink their blood. The flowers of the Masada bloom no longer than snow lies on the hills around Jerusalem. From the Masada, you can see the Lake of Asphalt. Look well at it, Eleazar! It is a lake as large as a sea and even the River Jordan cannot sweeten it: The waters are bitter and salt. You are that sea, Eleazar. So poisonous that no fish will swim in it, so foul that no bird builds its nest along your shores!"

Rachel's fury embarrassed me, for is not meekness the way of a woman? But Simon ben Judas smiled.

"I had asked them to give up Herod's fortress. I have no liking for that barren boast of a madman. If we Jews should make a last stand to give a fitting end to that book David's friend is composing, while he keeps house on Roman gold, I would say, let us fight for the waters of Ein-Gedi." Rabbi Simon paused and I wanted to protest that Joseph ben Matthias was no friend of mine; but Rabbi Simon recognized my anger and held up his hand. "The springs of Ein-Gedi are clear and the water sweet. They are like the Songs of David: they speak to the heart. Out of the ground of the Wilderness of Judea, they flow to make a garden in the desert. They conquer the desert, but only a part of it, as a prophet's words are lost in the shouting of the people. These waterfalls, these clear pools, should be our symbol, our teachers, not the nightmare of a madman!"

I looked at Rachel. She listened to Simon ben Judas not only with her ears but with her whole being.

I said nothing, for I did not agree. 'Judas Maccabeus made Judea a nation,' I thought. 'And the sword of Judas Maccabees is in the hand of Eleazar ben Ya'ir.'

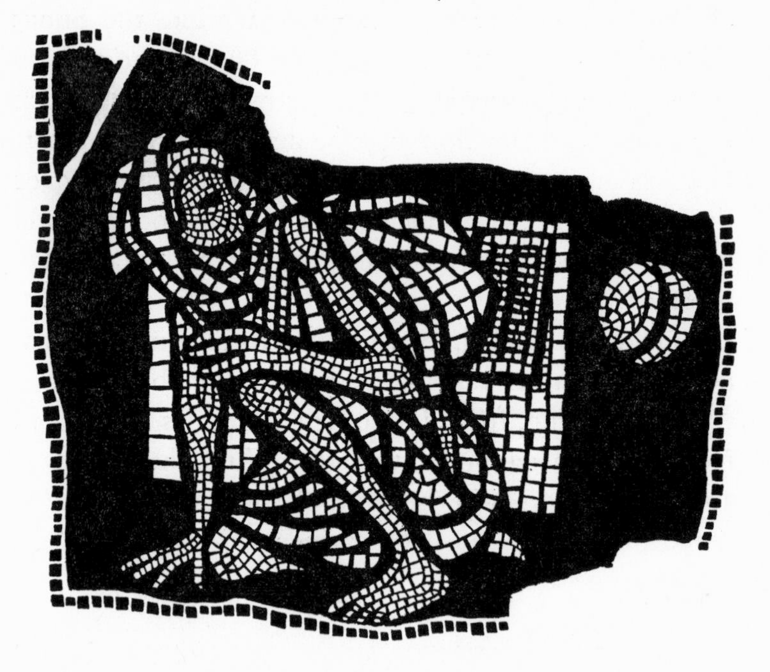

THE MONTH of Nisan passed, the summer sun began to show its strength, and the Passover Feast became a memory. It was the saddest Passover that I had ever observed. Few had the food to make the feast properly, and fewer could remember how to rejoice. Yet this is our strength. We Jews — we People of the Law — celebrate the calamities that have all but destroyed our nation. When we hear the story of our time in bondage, we remember that our forefathers had been slaves and that they became free. They ate the bread of affliction: the bitter bread, that is as wheat is to the chaff. And we gather strength from tears shed in the distant past, and the furrows on our faces caused by the troubles of today disappear. Other nations celebrate their victories, the Romans do and so do the Greeks. But we celebrate our belief in the Holy One: Blessed be His Name . . . and our wish, our strong wish to survive.

After the message had come from the Masada, Rachel seldom spoke to me or to anyone. She did her work, but her face was as closed as a shuttered house. I tried many times to speak with her, for it is not good for a person to carry sorrow alone. But perhaps I was too young to have understood her sorrow; for I remembered that as a child I had found none who understood mine.

One morning Rachel disappeared. She had left no message but we knew where she had gone. Her disappearance was discovered at noon and Rabbi Simon sent a man on horseback to Bethlehem to try to find her. He returned in the evening without even the slightest bit of information.

"She must travel through the wilderness of Judea to get to the Masada," Rabbi Simon began. "But I am not so afraid of the desert as of the soldiers she could meet. Many of those who call themselves Roman soldiers are nothing but bandits. What does a Jewish woman mean to them? At home they will lock their doors and with virtuous faces protect their daughters, but here they are like dogs." Simon ben Judas paced his room as he spoke. The object of his anger was alternately the Romans and Eleazar ben Ya'ir. "Oh, how I hate men who rejoice in their own strength, and do not recognize the weakness of their cause!" Against Rachel, Rabbi Simon uttered not a word.

"Let me go and find her," I pleaded.

"In the darkest times, David, Our People will need every little light that can give them hope. You are a little lamp; and as the filled lamp has many hours burning, so you have many years to live. I would not have Eleazar extinguish you because of his need for glory."

All day I walked through the ruins of Jerusalem, thinking of my loyalty to Rabbi Simon, whom I loved, and my desire to go to the Masada and join its defenders. In the late afternoon, I was beyond the destroyed walls, at a place near the Roman camp. As I approached it, I saw a number of crosses.

During a war, cruelty that in a period of peace would be thought unbearable is hardly noticed. The sight of crosses in Judea no longer caused a look of suffering in the faces of the passersby. I do not know what caused me to approach these crosses, for I did not want to see the tormented bodies. It was several days since they had died and the sight was horrible. On the fourth cross hung Saul! Usually those to be crucified were allowed to wear a loincloth — their clothes the Roman soldiers sold — but Saul was so poor that beneath his rags he had not worn one. His thin boy's body was naked.

"That will teach the Judean dog not to steal."

I shuddered. A soldier had walked up behind me. I turned to look at him. He was just a soldier, no more brutish than any other. I said nothing. I turned my back and walked quickly to the house of Simon ben Judas. Now I knew that I could not stay in the city. I would have to go to the Masada even if it meant that one day I, too, would be crucified.

At the marketplace in the Lower City I bought a knife with a good blade, which I slipped beneath my outer garments.

My father had sent Simon ben Judas money with which he had bought me clothes. My clothes were not of the finest linen, as I had worn in Tyre, for Rabbi Simon explained that the best linen and the cloths of the East, which are as light as butterfly's wings, are not worn on the body but on the soul, and though one's body should be covered in the sight of the Lord, one's soul should always be naked. I decided to take no extra clothes with me. Those that I would wear were my everyday garments and not those I put on for the Sabbath. In a linen bag I packed some dried lamb's meat and two breads. I took a waterskin for the trip through the desert. What little money I had — two shekels, a few half shekels, and some copper coins — I would take with me.

At first I had planned to leave as Rachel had, early in the morning; but as I turned the plan round and round in my mind I realized that I would be quickly missed, and Simon ben Judas would guess at once in which direction to send out people to search for me. Although it was both more difficult and more dangerous, I decided to leave at night.

Rabbi Simon retired early. He slept badly and would often get up during the night to read or copy, but he never came to my room to wake me. He said that the young needed sleep in order to prepare themselves for life, whereas the old needed to be awake to prepare themselves for death.

It had been dark very long and everything was quiet. I could not go through the gate because there was a watchman in the courtyard. In one of the warehouses there was an opening in an outer wall which faced a narrow lane; it was meant for the delivery of hay for the animals. It had shutters which were closed from the inside. When I opened them and looked down, I realized that the drop to the lane was so great that I would not be able to reach up and close the shutters. Open shutters would be an invitation to a thief — or worse. I looked up and down the narrow lane; the moon shone brightly. I saw a stick, probably dropped from a donkey who had carried wood; with its aid, I should be able to close the shutters.

I swung my legs out and, holding tightly onto my bundle, I jumped. I landed on all fours, and it seemed to me that I had made a lot of noise. I stood still and listened but all was silent. Standing on tiptoe, I managed with a stick to close the shutters, so that from the outside they did not appear to be unbarred.

The Romans had declared that no one might leave his house after dark; and though they were quite lenient during the first part of the night, those found later were heavily punished. True, most of the soldiers could be bribed, but I had not enough money for such a cloak of invisibility. Avoiding the larger streets and keeping in the shadows, I made my way in the direction of the road to Bethlehem. Although most of the walls were destroyed, the gates still stood and the Romans kept them guarded. The moonlight made it possible for me to climb the mountain of rubble which once had been the walls of our city, but it also made me fearful of being seen.

I heard soldiers and, while my heart beat so loudly that I thought all Jerusalem must be able to hear it, I lay still until they faded away in the distance. The top of the huge pile of rocks and bricks was broader than I had guessed it to be. In the blanching light of the moon, I crawled across it. On my way down on the other side, I fell and the stones and masonry slid with me. When I reached the ground, I got up and ran which was probably foolish. It was only luck that I was not caught.

Before the cock crowed, I was near Bethlehem. I walked around the city until I found a path that would take me to the village of Tekoa. I hoped to reach there shortly after sunrise. There I would rest and ask about Rachel. This was the most reasonable route for her to have taken. From Tekoa, she would surely try to find her way to the Lake of Asphalt and follow its shore to Ein-Gedi and the Masada. Though this was a longer trip, it was the most logical way for someone to travel who did not know the country.

I had always wanted to see the springs of Ein-Gedi, where David had hidden from Saul. It was in a cave near Ein-Gedi that David found King Saul sleeping, and cut a strip of his cloak to show the suspicious king that he might have killed him had this been his desire.

The sun had been up long when I finally reached the village. I was very tired, for I was unused to walking so far, and the strap of one of my sandals had broken.

The people of Tekoa were shepherds. They were silent men who were used to being alone. I went to the sandal maker, not only because I wanted a pair of sandals more suited to the rocks and cliffs of the wilderness, but because sandal makers usually were talkative. They were also inquisitive and this one was no exception.

"You have come from Jerusalem?" I nodded but said nothing. "And what brings you to Tekoa?"

Hesitantly, I asked, "Did a woman from Jerusalem pass through your village yesterday?"

The man raised his head. "A sandal maker hardly ever sees the sun, except on the Sabbath. How should I know if a strange woman passed through our village?"

Since the beginning of the war, a stranger was suspect. How could one know that he was an honest man and not a robber, or a spy for the Romans? I smiled and for once hoped that my looking young for my age would convince the sandal maker to speak with me. "She is my sister. They say that a sandal maker has as many eyes as he has visitors."

The man sought my glance to indicate that he would not dispute me, as well as to decide whether he cared to answer my questions. "The day before yesterday," he began sourly, "soldiers came and took two men away from this village . . . This morning just as the sun came up — and I had said my prayers — a woman came through the village. No one spoke to her for even a Jewish woman could have a Greek heart. It is shameless for a woman to travel alone . . . An old woman, her name is Miriam, cursed her and threw a stone at her . . . Miriam is toothless and hates the young. I don't think anyone else harmed her."

I felt certain that the woman must have been Rachel and I was angry. "Did not Naomi and Ruth travel from the land of the Moabs alone, and none threw stones at them or called them shameless?"

The sandal maker mockingly bowed his head. "Oh, Rabbi, blessed with wisdom, the women of this poor village are neither like Ruth or Naomi, so we let them not travel alone, for fear that their foolishness might hurt our honor. But we are but simple people and our manners are as crude as our workmanship." With this, he handed me the sandals.

Another person entered and looked at me suspiciously. I paid for the sandals and bid the sandal maker God's peace.

I had intended to stay and rest at the well; but now I thought that the mountains would be friendlier than the villagers, and after I had filled my waterskin, I walked on. I went in the direction that the sun rises from and did not stop until I could no longer see Tekoa.

I ate and drank a little of the water. The stillness of the wilderness surrounded me. Each of the mountains looked like the others: barren and desolate.

"Rachel! Rachel!" I cried out. And though I knew that she could not be near enough to hear me, I listened for an answer.

From far away came the hoarse cry of a bird: "Rahhhh . . . Rahhhh . . ."

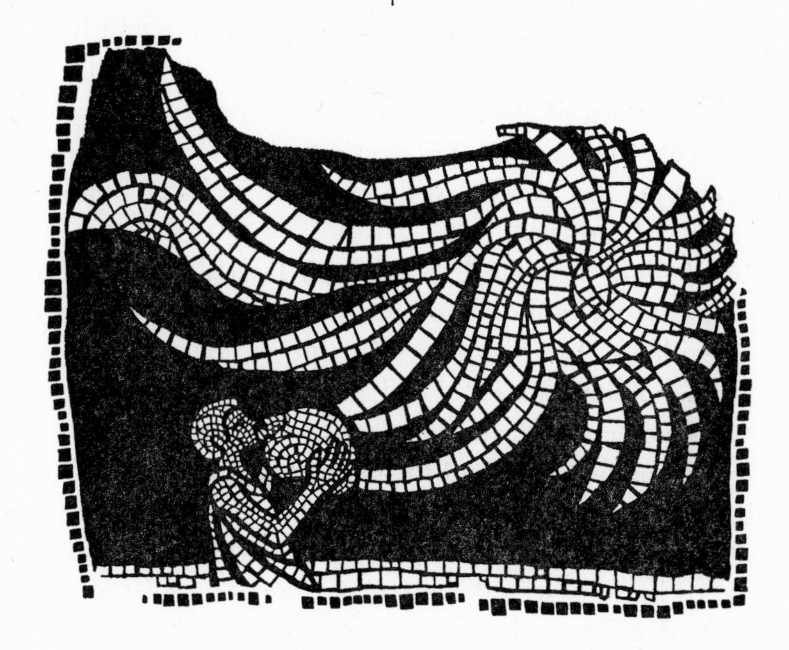

AT SUNRISE and at sunset the wilderness of Judea takes from the sun the color of fire. The mountains are red as if they are aflame; then as the twilight comes to the valleys, the mountaintops change from bright orange-red to the deep red of the embers of a fire. When the embers die, darkness creeps out from behind each rock, to tell you that you are alone.

The fear in your heart forms the shape of the shadows and the silence speaks. God draws near, for in the wilderness and the desert nature does not hide Him. The stars and the moon rule the night, as the sun does the day. Trees can protect you from the sun and hide you, at night, from the pale moon. But in the wilderness of Judea no green trees grow to embrace you and whisper, "We are alive as you are. We shall live long after you die. Come, little brother, and rest underneath our crowns."

All night I walked. Sometimes I would pick up a stone and throw it just to hear the noise of its fall break the stillness. I started down a ravine and fell. Although I had not hurt myself I did not get up. I listened as the stones and rocks that my fall had set tumbling down finally found rest; then I turned on my back and looked up at the stars.

'If I should die now,' I thought, 'no one would find me. The stars would look at me at night and the sun in the day, but no human eyes would see me ever again.' This thought made me feel that pity which turns inward, and is to real pity as copper is to gold.

"Mother . . . Mother . . . ," I called and I started to cry. Slowly the tears cleansed my heart as the spring floods clean the riverbeds, and all fear left me.

"The fool seeks gold and the clever man wisdom. The fool spends his days searching for gold, and his nights guarding it — for in all the corners of the world, thieves are standing — and envy is his only friend . . . The wise man spends his day seeking wisdom, and in the evening, he shares his thoughts like wine with his friends. He does not give of his wealth, but shareth it, and in adversity need not turn the eye towards the ground with shame . . . Though he rejoices in the melody of the harp and the companionship of friends, he fears not the night nor the loneliness of the desert." All these words ran through my mind as sheep that pass through a gate. They were thoughts that Simon ben Judas had spoken, and it astonished me that I could recall them.

I closed my eyes and the stars disappeared. I saw Rabbi Simon sitting in his room. I smiled and thought, 'I can make whatever world I want. I am master of this night, master of these hills.'

I got up and, glancing at the sky, I said, "Oh pale moon, you scare me not. Blinking star, I fear you not. And as for you, mountains: you are stones and rocks and nothing more." The words I had spoken to the mountains, I had shouted. I picked up three stones and threw them, and heard them bounce against their brothers.

The sun came up and lent its color to the world around me. The winds were still and no bird greeted the light. I followed the descent of the ravines, knowing that here all water runs towards the Lake of Asphalt. Sometimes in the spring it rains so heavily that raging rivers appear as if by magic; and as the magic rivers — the dream rivers — their life is very short. But the paths that the rainwater has made make it easy to travel in the wilderness of Judea, for they spell out the direction of the Lake of Asphalt.

In the afternoon, I saw for the first time the Lake of

Asphalt. It is very large, more like a sea than a lake, and maybe this is why it is also called the Sea of Salt. Its colors are blue and green. Some places near the shore its water glittered as a precious stone. I did not know then that my eyes should come to rest upon it so often that they would not see it. That day it seemed to me wondrous that I should be looking down at the Sea of Salt.

It was farther away than I had supposed and the sun was setting when I came near it. The cliffs which lead down to the shore were at this point very high. It was too late to try to descend. I ate and prepared myself for my second night alone. When the darkness brought out the stars, I was ready for sleep; and though the ground was hard, I slept without dreams the whole night through.

The light woke me. I was bewildered. Where was I? Perhaps I had expected to wake in the house of Simon ben Judas, or even my father's home in Tyre; for was not walking through the wilderness and seeing the Lake of Asphalt like a dream?

I drank some water and spilled a little on my hand to rub the sleep out of my eyes. After I had eaten I decided to try to find a place where I could get down to the shore more easily. I walked south and soon found a ravine which I could follow.

The first thing I did was throw a stone into the water. It said *plop* very much as the sea near my home in Tyre says when a stone greets it. I took a large rock, but this also was a disappointment. The stones nearest the lake were covered with salt. I scraped it off and tasted it. It was bitter and did not taste like the salt I was used to. I took off my sandals and waded; then I quickly returned to the pebbled beach and took off my clothes.

In Tyre, as any fisherman's son, I had learned to swim, in spite of my mother's terror of water and complaint that no other merchant's son could swim.

The stones at the bottom of the lake were very slippery, and when the water reached my knees, I sat down. The feeling of the water against my skin was very different from that of the sea; it felt almost like oil when you rub it on your hands. I swam a few strokes. It was strange to have trouble keeping my legs and feet beneath the water. I turned on my back and lay perfectly still. It was as if an invisible hand were holding me up from below. I started to swim back towards the beach, and it was then that I got a little water in my eyes.

The pain was sharp and I could not see. I swallowed a little of the water; it tasted foul. My feet searched for the bottom. It was shallow and I stood up. I rubbed my eyes with my hands and the pain became worse. I stumbled onto the shore. I searched with squinting eyes through which I could hardly see for my waterskin. I held it up high and poured water into my eyes and over my face, forgetting that it was drinking water I was spilling. When the pain finally lessened, I lowered the skin, and I realized that I had used almost all the water.

How far was it to Ein-Gedi with its springs? Was there no oasis before? Had I used it wisely there would have been enough water for two days and now there was hardly more than what would fill a small bowl.

Very quickly the sun dried my body, but my skin felt uncomfortable and all the little cuts on my legs smarted. As I dressed, I looked out over the Sea of Salt. It seemed to me to have changed. When I had first seen it from the cliffs, it had attracted me; it was the sea of my wishes, the sea of my dreams. Now it repelled me. In it there were no fish one could catch, no water one could drink or even refresh oneself with, as the waters of the sea.

"You are useless," I said, and threw a rock into it as if I were punishing it.

My mouth was so filled with salt that I wanted to drink very much; but I only took a large swallow, and this I kept in my mouth as long as possible before letting it slide down my throat.

"You have robbed me of my water," I said to the lake.

As the Sea of Salt would not answer, I answered for it, "I have not! You treated me as if I were filled with fresh water. The fault was not mine, it was yours, for I was only true to my nature."

I laughed. Now I had begun to feel happy again and when I looked back at the Sea of Salt, it no longer frightened me. "You are right and I shan't swim in you any more," I called.

Speaking for the lake, I said, "I don't care, it is all the same to me."

Between the place where I had swum in the Sea of Salt and Ein-Gedi, there were no springs of fresh water; but the distance to Ein-Gedi was not as far as I had feared. I had supposed that I would not reach it before the following day. At noon when the sun was burning hot I had taken only two mouthfuls of water, though I suffered terribly from thirst.

The sun was still above the mountains when I arrived at Ein-Gedi.

"The waters of Ein-Gedi!" The words are honey in the mouth. Ein-Gedi is soft like the fleece of a lamb, wondrous like the fulfillment of a dream. In the marketplace in Jerusalem I had heard a shepherd talk of it. "Ein-Gedi is like a young girl who walks through the market and makes the old men forget their age." Some people who had never seen Ein-Gedi laughed at him; but an old man nodded and said, "When you rest by the pools of Ein-Gedi, you have no age. Surely, when God took the Garden of Eden from us, he gave us Ein-Gedi so that we might know what we had lost."

If Ein-Gedi is a young woman, as the shepherd said, she is shy; and if you come from the north she guards herself with a little cape of steep rocks. And even after you have climbed the cape and come down on the other side, you can only see on the plain that now opens before you a few trees and some bushes. My disappointment was very great!

"They have told me lies," I thought; then suddenly, by chance, I glanced away from the sea towards the mountains. I saw that the nearest mountain was cleaved and through it ran a valley; and there the rocks were hidden by greenness! As I neared the valley I could hear water running. On a bush I saw a tiny bird with bright feathers. I ran towards the sound of the water. The little bird flew up. There hidden by the bushes was a clear stream. I kneeled down by it and drank. I pushed my face into the stream until my whole head was wet.

"Shalom," someone said behind me.

I raised my head; the water from my hair was running down my back. "Shalom," I said and looked at the stranger.

THE MAN was dressed as a shepherd, but his clothes were clean and I guessed that he was one of a group of Essenes whom I had heard lived near Ein-Gedi.

"I come from Jerusalem and am on my way to the Masada," I said while with my hands I tried to dry my face.

"The sun will dry you."

I stopped rubbing my face and waited; but the man said no more. "How far is it to the Masada?" I asked.

The man turned and looked south. "Too far for to-day. Strangers are not treated kindly if they come after sunset; but if you start in the morning, you can be at the foot of the mountain before noon. Why do you want to go to the Masada, are you a soldier?"

"I am a student, a follower of Rabbi Simon ben Judas in Jerusalem."

"Is this part of the teachings of your master, that his pupils should go wandering in the wilderness?"

He smiled and held his head cocked to one side while he waited for my answer. I have never liked persons who use words in this manner. I always grew angry when my Greek teacher in Tyre would say, if my lesson had not been learned properly, "I see, David, you have prepared yourself well today." And now when I turned to the Essene, I spoke more forcefully than I had intended. "To be alone in the desert with God harms no man but the fool who thinks that the sun is set in the sky to cast his shadow."

He grinned to show that my anger could not reach him. "You have not answered my question. Why are you going to the Masada?"

I concentrated my gaze upon the pool until my annoyance was controllable. "I am seeking a woman. Her name is Rachel. She has gone to the Masada because her brother is there and her brother's children."

"And why do you, a student of the Torah, seek a woman?"

I kept my eyes on the water. "And why do you, a stranger, seek information that does not concern you, as a hen seeks a grain of wheat?" I glanced up at him; he was no longer smiling.

"And is this the manner you answer your master?"

I was already sorry that I had let my anger run away with my tongue. I met his gaze and said, "No, but Rabbi Simon ben Judas has only one tongue, and his words have only one meaning . . . God's tongue is not forked; and therefore, ours should not be so . . . I seek this woman because she is alone. She lost her children and her husband in the fall of Machærus. She has been to me as an older sister, and I have traveled through the wilderness as a brother who has lost a sister."

The man looked up towards the sky. 'He knows something. Rachel has been here,' I thought.

"Last evening, just before sunset, a woman came here. She was fed and she slept here. She left this morning." He looked down towards the Sea of Salt. "She did not say where she came from, nor that her husband and children had died."

Speaking softly — for now my anger was gone — I said, "What woman of Israel need tell of her tears today? Is there a mother in all of Judea who has not followed a child or the father of her children to a grave? The Romans at Machærus forbid the people to bury their dead. Seven evenings the sun set on the dead, and seven mornings it rose to shed light on them; then the Roman commander had them burned and their ashes spread over the fields. Rachel has not buried her husband, and therefore he is unburied in her heart as well." I saw that my words hurt the Essene, and though I felt ashamed of it my heart rejoiced.

The people who belong to the Essene sect care much for the Law. An Essene would rather have his hand cut off than light a fire on the Sabbath. The thought of Jews lying unburied must have been almost unbearable to this man.

"You may eat and sleep here. We have a hut for strangers," he said almost humbly. I thanked him and he explained that kindness towards strangers and travelers had been commanded by God. He led me to a hut which was empty except for a bed of leaves. "Food will be brought to you here, for strangers cannot eat at our table."

I felt strange, for I knew that to this man I was unclean. I thanked him again and he replied, "I am but a tool. The hand is the Lord's and to Him you should offer your thanks."

His remarks irritated me but I tried not to show it. In my mind I recalled that Simon ben Judas held the piety of the Essenes in contempt. He had said that an Essene was humble towards God, as a Roman slave was to his Emperor. But a moment later, when the man began to speak of Ein-Gedi — of the plants that grew there, and of the birds and other animals that lived there — I was reminded of how Miriam, the teacher's daughter who had been with my father's caravan, had spoken of the fig tree that had grown in front of her house in Jerusalem. And I realized that the Essenes were simple people and it might have been their simplicity that caused Simon ben Judas' disgust — he, who was so learned.

The Essene looked up at the sun to judge how long it would be before it set, then he offered to show me the way to the waterfall.

We walked into the cleft; it is too narrow to be called a valley and some places it is very steep. The path follows the water, and there are small waterfalls and pools along the way. Reeds grow tall and the world is green; but if you should but raise your eyes to the mountains, the barren rock is all that will greet them. "Up there." My guide pointed to the southern mountainside. "There are springs and pools. Most of us live up there, but our guests are asked to sleep down in the house by the Lake of Asphalt."

I looked up; I could see a few trees at the very top of the mountain, for it was not very high. The other side of the cleft, where the mountain ended in ragged peaks, was desolate.

"How many are you up there?" I asked.

He did not answer, but merely pointed ahead. "If you follow the path you will come to the large waterfall; but please, return before nightfall." He disappeared among the reeds, and the sound of the water filled my ears so that I could not hear his footsteps.

'Surely they live only for God,' I thought. No man

among the Essenes has property of his own. They live in poverty and think that man's sole duty on earth is to keep the Laws of the Torah. Their lives are a secret to us, for they consider both Pharisees and Sadducees unclean, and will not mix with us.

"God led us out of the desert and now the Essenes will lead us back into it. God made a Covenant with us, but the Essenes think themselves so pure that they can make a Covenant with God. Beware, David, of a man who is too humble, for his arrogance is so great that he needs hide it." The words were of Simon ben Judas. I felt a little shamed for having recalled them now for tonight I would sleep in the Essenes' hut and eat their food.

The song of the water drew me further and further. Once I walked across a stream and the water felt cold against my feet. I climbed over a rock and there it was: the waterfall.

The cleft had ended in a wall of rock, and from high above the water fell into the pool. First it fell freely, then it slid down through a hollow green with ferns before it made its final descent into the pool. I kneeled at the edge; the water was clear and each little stone beneath the surface could be seen. It was neither large nor deep. I took off my sandals. Only where the water fell did it reach my knees. It was cool and I wanted to swim.

I took off my clothes and entered the pool again. Everything about me was in shadow, but high above the mountains glistened red in the light of the setting sun. Near where the water fell I started to swim, but I was in awe of the magic and it frightened me. I stood up almost at once.

Halfway up to the top of the mountain was one of the wild goats that live around Ein-Gedi. It stood perfectly still, its neck bent, its head thrown back as if it were contemplating the mountaintop. I waded to the water's edge and sat down upon a rock to wait for my body to dry, so I could put my clothes on again.

The thought that had followed me as a shadow came to me: 'What are you, David?'

I trembled, not only because I was cold but also because I could not understand why I wanted an answer to that question. Why did it matter to me to know? Why could I not have stayed with my father in Tyre and become a wine merchant? My father had not sent me away, as Abraham had Ishmael. No, I had gone by myself; and that shadow, that question had led me. To know yourself, is it not vanity?

I got up. I was dry, but I did not put on my clothes; I bent forward to see myself in the waters of the pool. A boy's face, below a mass of uncombed hair, looked back at me. No beard, only a little hair above the lip. I disturbed the water with my hand and the face disappeared. I rose and put on my clothes.

It was near sunset when I came back to the hut. A bowl of lentils had been left for me. I ate outside and watched the sun disappear behind the mountains. I returned to the hut, prayed, and lay down to sleep. But sleep would not come as a mother and fold me in its arms. Not before the moon had long been up did my eyes finally close and time disappear.

THE MASADA | 22

IN THE MORNING, after eating the bread and drinking the goat's milk which the Essenes had given me, I left Ein-Gedi, following the shore of the Sea of Salt. Soon the mountains fell away and a large desolate plain separated the mountains and the lake. A half hour beyond Ein-Gedi, it became a memory. Time and again I looked back. Only a few trees remained and the sight of them could not conjure the vision of the waterfalls and pools. "It was a dream," I said to myself and looked ahead along the barren shores of the Lake of Asphalt.

Though noon had not yet come, the sun was burning hot. I saw a group of men coming towards me. I knew they must have seen me. There were about twenty of them. The two who walked in front wore swords on their left side — not on their right, as the Romans did.

"Shalom . . . Peace . . ." I called and waited for them.

No one answered. But when they reached me, they formed a circle around me, as if they expected me to try to escape. Their faces were burned by the sun and all of them carried arms: some had bow and arrow, some a sling, and all had daggers at their sides. I knew they were men from the Masada, for the history of the war was written on their faces.

"Are you Eleazar ben Ya'ir?" I asked the taller of the two men who wore swords.

My question made them all laugh and their laughter made their faces appear less unfriendly. The man whom I had mistaken for Eleazar ben Ya'ir asked who I was. I answered that I was a follower of Simon ben Judas and that I knew one of the men on the Masada. "He is called Joab," I explained, "and he has come several times to speak with my master."

"Are you a messenger from Jerusalem?"

"I have come to join you," I said.

Some of the men smiled more kindly towards me, but one of the officers, who until now had not spoken, said in a tone filled with contempt, "Why?" When I didn't answer immediately, he added an insult to his question, "Are we to get all the babes of Jerusalem before they are weaned?"

Some of the men laughed; and in order not to see their faces while I phrased my answer, I looked at the ground. "The war has weaned many babies, death having taken the mother's breast out of their mouths and given them as nurse, hunger. But my bar mitzvah was over a year ago and according to Our Law, I am a man." Now I stared into the officer's face.

He returned my glance without a word; then he turned his back on me, as if I no longer interested him. To one of his men he said, "Take him back. If he should attempt to run, kill him." Then he walked away in the direction of Ein-Gedi. The others looked at me curiously; then they followed him, all except the one who had been ordered to take me to the Masada.

"You were lucky."

The voice startled me. My attention had been on the men walking away, and momentarily I had forgotten the one who had been left behind to kill me, if need be. "Why?" I asked.

"Because that was Isaac ben Joseph and he thinks that your master, Simon ben Judas, is a traitor . . . He thinks that all men who are not on the Masada are traitors."

My guard was no longer young. His hair was graying. A scar crossed his right cheek from beneath his eyes to his mouth; and yet his face was pleasant, for he smiled almost constantly. "He is as great a soldier as

Eleazar ben Ya'ir and fears no one." I nodded as a pupil who is learning his lessons does when his teacher explains a rule which may not be disputed. "And yet compared to Eleazar, he is like the dove to the eagle."

'He is trying to frighten me,' I thought. Aloud I asked, "Who was the man . . . the one whom I thought was Eleazar?"

He laughed. "His name is Ezra ben Seth, but he is called Ezra the Runner — though not to his face. He is braver at home than in the battlefield; but he is a clever man and he talks well at meetings. His sword may not be dangerous but his tongue is . . . Come." He started to walk, taking long strides which made it difficult for me to keep up with him. He asked me about Jerusalem: how many had died there? And if the Temple had been completely destroyed. Of the Roman army, too, he wanted to know much: how many soldiers there were and the names of the commanders. I answered as best I could, and he seemed satisfied, as though I was confirming what he himself already knew.

"My name is Dan," he said; then he lifted his arm and pointed to a mountain. "There is the Masada."

"Is that the Masada?" My voice told of my disappointment. I do not know what I had expected, but from where we stood it looked like any other mountain. I think I had dreamt of tall towers and great walls, not understanding that the strength of the Masada lay not so much in its battlements as in the fact that it was, indeed, a mountain. As I strained my eyes, I could make out walls and towers; but the walls were low and the square towers not very much higher.

"It is a fortress, not a temple or palace, though Herod the Great called it one . . . No one can take the Masada; it is invincible," Dan assured me confidently.

"Where were they going?"

"Do not ask questions like that," he answered me threateningly, "or people will think you are a fool or a spy . . . or both."

Lately, the people of the Masada had made several raids on small Roman garrisons; and in Jerusalem, we had smiled happily when we heard the news. "They will come here," I said, "to revenge themselves."

"The Greeks are welcome," he replied, though he too was referring to the Roman army. "We shall kill as many of them as their commanders in Jerusalem care to send," he boasted.

I realized that he had no idea of the strength of Rome, and that what Simon ben Judas had said was true: "In the wilderness, David, the Zealots are masters and I fear that their ignorance has made them arrogant." But as I began to get a better view of the Masada, I understood them. From the plain below, the sides of the mountain rose almost straight up, while the summit was flat. It looked as though God had cut off the top with a great knife.

"Let us rest. From now on we must climb like goats." Dan sat on the ground and I threw myself down beside him. We were at the foot of the Masada, and the path up its side, with its winding curves, looked like the body of a huge snake.

"They say that Herod built it because he did not trust the people of Judea." Dan had his back to the mountain and was looking out over the Sea of Salt. "Herod was not a Jew. He did not keep the Law." Dan spoke these words matter-of-factly, as if he were talking of the weather; and I realized that to him Herod the Great meant nothing.

How often I had thought of the crimes of Herod, and yet I could not dismiss him as a Roman — though he had been more that than he had been a Jew. But I had been in Caesarea and my father was a rich man.

"If you feel your feet sliding, use your hands and crawl on all fours!" Dan shouted at me, at a point where the path was very narrow and the mountain fell sheer.

I glanced down. We were almost on top, and everything below seemed tiny and very far away. 'No army would ever be able to use that path to conquer the Masada,' I thought. 'One archer from the wall could hold it against all the armies of Rome.' I looked ahead towards the gate; the portals were open, two men were standing guard. 'If one lives in an eagle's nest, can one avoid believing that one is an eagle?' I asked myself.

"What have you brought, Dan?" one of the guards called.

Dan shouted, "We caught a Greek general. He had disguised himself as a boy." The laughter of the other men made me understand that Dan was a buffoon of whom a joke was expected.

The path ended in steps that had been cut into the rock. I had been walking bent forward, now I had to straighten myself. I tried to look as dignified as possible.

"The Roman generals are small, eh, Dan?"

"They grow them that way to make it harder for an arrow to hit them," he answered. "Their king is so small that they keep him in a pot, so the mice won't eat him." Pointing to me he said, "He says that he's got friends in Jerusalem. We'll see if he has."

I looked angrily at Dan, for I had thought we had become friends, and now he was betraying me.

"He can sleep in the cell, until Eleazar decides what to do with him," Dan continued. We had entered the guardroom and, in spite of my situation, I noted what a relief it was to be out of the sun. I lifted my waterskin to my lips and drank. Dan started to laugh and I stopped. I turned around, Dan was leaving. I looked at him and he stared back at me but he said nothing.

"Come on," one of the guards ordered.

For a moment I didn't realize that he was talking to me. He grabbed my arm. I drew away, but his grasp was strong. Before I knew what was happening, he had dragged me out into the sunshine again.

"Let me go!" I screamed, for I have never liked anyone to touch me. The man laughed as he pushed me before him. We had gone only a few steps when we came to a little door in the wall. He opened it and threw me inside.

"I want to see Eleazar ben Ya'ir!" I shouted as the door was barred.

"You will," the guard replied, and I heard him walk away.

I LOOKED with fury at the locked door. I banged on it with my fist, but no one came. The room was tiny. A light fell from a small opening in the outer wall. Far below I could see the Lake of Asphalt and the mountains beyond it. Evening came. I watched the mountains turn red and the sea darken.

In the corner was a bed made of twigs and straw. I lay down and waited. Every time someone went to or from the guardroom I could hear it. At sunset the gates were closed, and I listened to the noises of the big beam being placed across to lock them.

As the room grew dark I thought, 'Surely Dan must have told about me by now. Why has no one come to get me?' I had not quite forgotten what Joseph ben Matthias had said of the Zealots, that they were a bunch of cutthroats and bandits; and I was afraid. 'You must be brave,' I told myself. 'You must not show your fear. They will not harm you. Are they not Keepers of the Law? Soldiers of Judea, Jews like yourself?'

When first I heard the scratching at the door, I thought it was a mouse; but then my name was whispered, "David . . . David."

I jumped up and ran to the little door. I kneeled down. "Rachel?" I said eagerly.

"Not so loud," she whispered. "I can only stay a moment. Tomorrow they will bring you to Eleazar . . . You will get no food tonight. It's his idea; he wants to test you, frighten you a little. But he knows who you are. I have told him that your father is a rich merchant in Tyre and that you are a friend of Joseph ben Matthias; and I think he is pleased that you've come. But he is hard and he enjoys fear in others."

"I shan't be afraid," I whispered back.

"Did Simon ben Judas send you?"

I shook my head but then I laughed, remembering that Rachel could not see me. "No, I came by myself." My words were greeted by silence and I thought Rachel had gone away. "Rachel . . . Rachel . . . ," I whispered.

"Little fool," she answered and her voice was filled

with tenderness. "Good night and don't be afraid."

"Good night," I whispered back; then I heard her get up and walk away.

For a while I stood at the door. I heard laughter from the guardroom and the voices of people talking in the distance. Through the slit in the wall, I looked once more at the sky; the stars were out. Before I went to sleep I prayed. I closed my eyes and thought of Tyre; as I grew more drowsy, of Simon ben Judas; and at last, I saw again the pools of Ein-Gedi.

The sun was already in the sky when I woke. Its rays illuminated the wall next to the door and made the whitewash appear pink. I stretched myself and rubbed my eyes. With my hands I combed my hair.

"My name is David ben Joseph . . . I have slept through the night and my dreams have been blessed by the Lord," I said out loud as if there were someone in the room.

I was very hungry, which I tried not to notice. The guards had taken my waterskin and my thirst was not as easy to ignore as my hunger.

To me it seemed that I waited endlessly for someone to come, but when the door finally opened I was taken by surprise. I had been looking out over the Sea of Salt. I turned and the light from the open door blinded me. First the guard handed me my waterskin and kept his back to me while, in spite of myself, I drank greedily.

"Come," he ordered.

I made the man wait for a moment; then I stepped out into the sunlight. We passed a group of children playing; it seemed a curious sight in such a place but also a comforting one.

"How old are you?" the guard asked.

I looked at him carefully, I could not recall having seen him before. "Fifteen," I answered.

"You look younger," he said and grinned.

I shrugged my shoulders, as if to say, 'What do I care how young I look?' But the truth was that I did care and it irritated me that my beard would not grow.

The guard led me to a large building which had been part of King Herod's palace. The room we entered had a beautiful floor in which tiny stones had been inlaid to make intricate patterns, and the walls had been painted. Somehow the beauty appeared forsaken, as if it went unnoticed and unwanted.

Five men were sitting on the floor; they looked at me with open interest but they did not speak to me. In the corner a man was tending a fire; the smoke drifted out through a crudely made hole in the ceiling.

"Wait here," my guard said. He opened a door to an inner room. I tried to listen, for I thought that Eleazar ben Ya'ir was there; but I could hear nothing.

My guard came out quickly, leaving the door ajar. With a nod of his head, he indicated that I should go in. I glanced around the room: even the man who was tending the fire was watching me intently. I straight-ened myself and entered; nor did I turn around when the door was closed behind me.

Eleazar stood with his back to me, facing a wall; his hands were clasped behind him. I stepped as far as the table in the center of the room. On it were lying a scroll, an inkwell, and writing reeds.

"What is your name?" he asked without turning around. He was not tall, but his back was very broad. His hair was long and black, and well combed.

"David ben Joseph," I said trying to make my voice sound deep.

"David was a soldier, the greatest soldier the Children of Israel ever had."

I folded my hands across my chest. "David was also a poet, the greatest the Children of Israel ever had."

"One can hear that you are a friend of Joseph ben Matthias, the Commander of Jotapata." Slowly Eleazar turned around and looked at me.

'It is his eyes,' I thought. 'It is his eyes that people see when they look at him. They are like two knives: two daggers in his face.'

"Are you a poet, too?" he asked.

"No," I answered, "and I am not a soldier, either."

"Why have you come here, then?" His lips moved into a little smile. On his chest he was wearing a silver plate.

'He reminds me of one of the Greek actors I once saw in Tyre, who wore masks to hide their faces,' I thought. "If I had said I was a soldier, I would have been bragging. If I had said I was a poet, I would have been lying . . . If you will teach me, I shall become a soldier," I said slowly.

"Maybe I shall make a poet of you," he said mockingly.

"No," I replied. "You can teach a man to throw a stone with a sling. You can teach him what stone to choose. But you cannot teach him to become a prophet or a poet."

Eleazar looked annoyed. "I am sure Herod kept poets here, but I have little use for them."

I glanced down at the table and without intending to, I started to read the scroll that lay open. It was the Song of Solomon, and I could not help smiling.

Eleazar followed my gaze. "Turn it over," he ordered.

I took the scroll in my hand. It was good parchment. "The scribe has copied the Song well."

"Turn it over," he repeated.

On the other side of the parchment were written lists of names and numbers. Several of the names were strangely spelled and the ink used had been of inferior quality.

"Those are accounts. The numbers are for the rations issued to each man, according to how large a family he has."

I waited but Eleazar said no more. Hesitantly, I turned the scroll to read the Song:

"By night on my bed I sought him whom my soul loveth: I sought him, but found him not.

"I will rise now, and go about the city in the streets and in the broad ways I will seek him whom my soul loveth: I sought him, but found him not."

I had read the Song of Solomon many times before but I had not understood it. But at that moment the words, "*I sought him, but found him not,*" moved me strangely and I put the scroll back on the table.

"I understand that you are a scribe. I have need of you if your hand is steady with a reed."

"I shall do my best," I said. Eleazar ben Ya'ir caught my glance with his own severe gaze. Then he called the man who had been my guard and told him to find quarters for me among the single men, who lived by the west wall. To me he spoke no more, indicating with a wave of his hand that I should depart.

"You have done well," the man said, as soon as he had closed the door.

I smiled. I was thinking that now I knew Eleazar ben Ya'ir; and yet I understood him less than when he had been a name. "He wore a silver breastplate," I said.

"Yes, he always wears it. He took it from a Roman captain after he had killed him."

"It is very beautiful," I remarked.

With awe in his voice, my companion said, "The weight in silver is worth ten slaves."

HE TOLD ME that I could go back to Jerusalem, that he cared no more for my staying on the Masada than the fig tree cares for the frost of winter."

"And what did you say?" I asked smiling, for I knew the power of Rachel's tongue when she was angry.

"I said that he was a tyrant, not a leader; that he was worse than King Herod . . . That he had changed much for the worse since the time when we played together as children, that I hated him . . ."

I started to laugh. "Could you find anything more to say?"

"I could have gone on until the time for the evening prayers . . . but he hit me," she said and grinned.

I dared not look at her, for I was thinking, 'That is the only way to have stopped you, Rachel.'

Suddenly she became sad, "All I wanted was the children."

"Yes," I said gently, for I knew that she would do anything to get the children, and I wondered if it only was because her own had been killed. "But he still won't let them go?"

She shook her head angrily. "You don't understand, for you are a man, too — even though you still are a boy. I cannot bear that they should be killed before they have lived. The boy is four; the girl, five — almost the same ages that my children were. When a man sees his little son, he imagines him as an adult; but when a woman sees her son as a grown man, she still sees the child. She still remembers how she washed and dressed him when he was a baby; and her heart loves him passionately for what he was. A man loves his son because he may become wise, honored, or rich. And his daughter he loves most if she is beautiful because then she can marry well, and so bring him glory."

Rachel and I were sitting on the eastern wall of the Masada. I flipped the little stone that I had been holding in my hand over the wall. "How do you know that the children will die?"

"Do you think that the Romans will let you stay

here? They are only biding their time. They will come. They murdered the children in Machærus; do you think they will spare the children of the Masada?"

I did not answer. I was looking out over the Lake of Asphalt. Two Sabbaths had passed since I had come to the Masada and already the wilderness seemed to be the world; and I too believed that beyond the Sea of Salt, which I no longer looked at with amazement, there was no other world.

"He could send all the children away now; and the women, too. They could be taken to Jerusalem and nothing would happen to them. But Eleazar knows that if they go, the men will follow, and he will have to defend the Masada alone."

"If the Masada falls, all hope is gone," I said.

"He has snared you in his dream. You are as a caught bird and your neck will be broken!"

Half in anger and half in fun I said to Rachel, "You are a Greek."

"No," she replied firmly, "I am a woman."

I laughed. "A Greek woman."

Knowing that I was teasing her, Rachel smiled.

"Do you know," I said more seriously, "they called Simon ben Judas a Greek?"

"Who are they?" Rachel asked.

"The people in the street."

Rachel smiled contemptuously, "The people in the street are always calling names. They think that their tongues are made for shouting and their hands for throwing stones."

"There he is," I said softly. Eleazar ben Ya'ir with four other of the leaders of the Masada had just come out of the little palace that he used as a headquarters. The sun reflected on his silver breastplate. I looked at Rachel, expecting to see hate painted on her face; but to my surprise it was not.

"The fool," she said and her voice was more tender than disparaging.

Among the men I noticed Rachel's brother, and I wondered which of the two men she was talking about, Eleazar or her brother. "Whom do you call a fool?" I asked.

She understood at once what I meant. "My brother is a fool, too; but he is a fool's fool. He needs someone to follow; and he has followed Eleazar since he learned to walk."

I had never asked Rachel about her own husband. I knew nothing of him except that he had been a merchant and that she had not been allowed by the Romans to bury him. "Was your husband a fool, too?" I asked, but Rachel frowned and I regretted my question.

"He was a good man and he was not a fool."

A child appeared below us. It was Rachel's niece. I waved to the girl and she laughed up at me. I watched Rachel as she walked down the three steps from the wall. She moved as gracefully as one of the dancing figures on a Greek vase.

Now the little boy came. Both of the children ran to her and she took each by the hand. Out of the wall I loosened a small pebble and threw it after them. Rachel turned and shouted, mixed with laughter, "You are a fool, too . . . But a little one."

I returned to my work reluctantly, for I never tired of looking at the beauty of the wilderness. I was making an account of all the food in the storehouses of the Masada. It was not easy, for some of the supplies had been there for many years, and some of the wheat was so old I was not sure we could use it. But on the whole things kept well on the Masada because the air in the wilderness is so dry; some of the oil was from the time of King Herod.

We were a little over a thousand people on the Masada and we had enough food to withstand a siege of many years. We had meat and cheese, but fresh vegetables we seldom had in large quantities. Sometimes the raiders would return with a donkey load or two; but among a thousand people, a sack of pomegranates is not much. Still we lived so well that if people sometimes spoke of the fresh figs of Jerusalem, I think it was more the green tree they longed for than the fruit. Water we had in abundance. The system of cisterns which King Herod had constructed was such that thirty thousand soldiers could have lived on the Masada for a year without any of them knowing thirst.

I liked my work, for I was left to myself. I had a small room where I kept my writing materials and where I even had an oil lamp, so that after nightfall I could retire there.

The men of the Masada were organized into groups, but because of my special work I belonged to none. I slept with three other young men who were my own age or a little older. None of them was my friend and none my enemy. As many of those on the Masada, they could not write; and only one of them could read— and this with great difficulty. Towards my accomplishments their feelings were a mixture of disgust and respect. Disgust because strength was highly valued on the Masada and I was not strong nor had I learned to use either the bow or the sling well. But I spoke the language of the Torah and knew by heart large sections of it. The men of the Masada were Keepers of the Law and they respected all those who had knowledge.

The days resembled one another. Midsummer came, and the heat during the day, when no wind blew, was almost unbearable. Small groups of men went out on raids. Sometimes they came back not only with booty, but with their number increased: a shepherd or a young man who had fled from one of our cities to join us. But often wails of sorrow were heard from the women, telling that not all had returned.

I have said that the people of the Masada were Keepers of the Law; but they were more than that. "Zealots," some have called them; and sometimes they used the word themselves. Zealots they were. All the laws and rituals were carefully kept, and from this the men drew strength. Eleazar ben Ya'ir was their leader because they looked upon him as a Prophet sent by God. God was always near us on the Masada; and the Torah was not a tale of time past: We were the people of the Torah.

No, not *we*, but *they*, for though with all my heart I wanted to feel as my companions did, I could not. Not that I doubted God, the Most Holy One, the Bringer of Peace, but I doubted myself. In the midst of the prayers before sunset, my mind would wander from the words my mouth was uttering. I would look at my companions and think, 'They have no doubt that God will listen to their prayers, and I am not sure that I want him to listen to mine.'

THE PALACE OF KING HEROD THE GREAT | 25

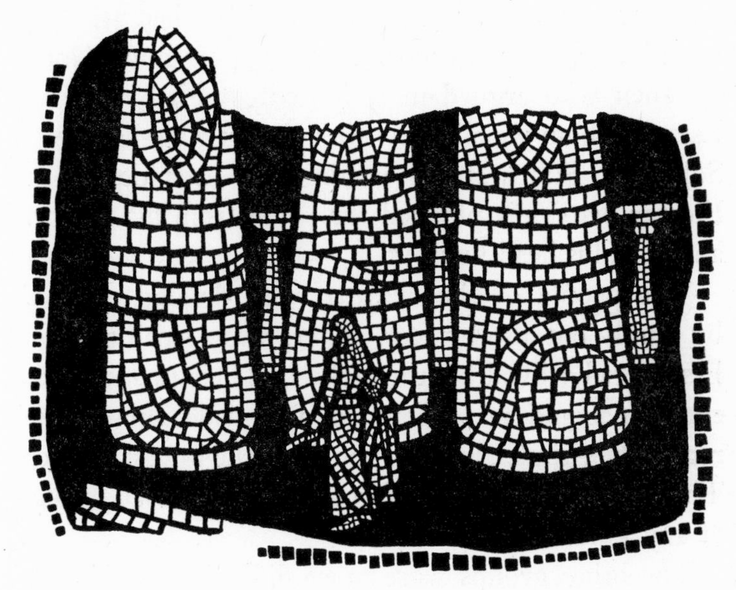

My work of making accounts of the stores on the Masada took a long time. I no longer used parchment but clay tablets. What little parchment we now had was used for sending messages to Jerusalem and other cities of Judea. In the beginning I had cut off the blank ends of several of the scrolls at the command of Eleazar; but his treatment of the scrolls was heavily censured in a meeting by one of the Levites. It is written that sacred writing must never be burned or destroyed; the scroll that had contained the Song of Solomon and which had been used for keeping accounts was buried now. Eleazar had had to explain his actions and defend them, which was unusual for him. At that meeting I had felt sorry for Eleazar, for no one dared to support him. One of the men who argued most heatedly with him was an Essene, whom we all knew thought little of the Song of Solomon. Still a sacred writing had been defiled and Eleazar ben Ya'ir plucked the pride from his forehead and bent his head humbly.

The people of the Masada were divided not only by family but also by sect. There was a small group of Essenes who lived by themselves. Their property was communal and no difference was made among their ranks; their leader lived as poorly as the lowest of them. Their women had clean faces and wore no adornment of any kind.

The other groups were more difficult to distinguish from each other. They were all Pharisees. Of Sadducees, there were none on the Masada. Among the Pharisees it was a matter of leadership — a particular officer whom each group followed — rather than any religious differences. Eleazar ben Ya'ir belonged to no group, and the men of the Masada could not have imagined another leader. He was their faith: their sun and their moon.

The Masada had been built by King Herod the Great; both the fortress and the palaces had been constructed at his command. But Eleazar and the Zealots inherited only the fortress, for the palaces were in ruins. There was a large one by the western wall, which was used without any regard for the remains of its former splendor. The palace which fascinated me was the one that had been cut out of the rock on the narrow northern tip. There were three terraces, one below the other, and they were connected by stairs.

The stairs to the lowest level were in ill repair and it was difficult to make the descent. The colonnades still stood, but the plaster that covered the columns was damaged. 'This,' I thought, 'is Herod. This is his arrogance. This is the spear he threw against death . . . "In the wilderness I shall build a palace. It shall have a colonnade, where one may walk in coolness, when the southern wind blows and dries the blood out of a man's body." '

This particular day was in winter. The sun was shining, and now at noon the air was pleasantly warm. I had thought of King Herod, but my daydreams had been words and I grew tired of them. Idly I watched a lizard and saw it disappear into a crack in one of the columns. The lizard is a strange animal and Judea is filled with them. They can live in the desert where man is a fear-filled traveler. Does it know of us? What does the lizard think when we cast a shadow across its path?

That day my interest in the lizard had been so intense that I had not heard the footsteps of someone approaching me. "What are you doing, little scribe?"

"Watching a lizard." Smiling, I lifted my head to look at Eleazar ben Ya'ir. Eleazar only called me "little scribe" when he was pleased with me. At other times, he called me a "merchant's son," a "Greek," or if he was really angry he would say, "friend of that traitor, Joseph ben Matthias!" Then I too would be angry and we would part, I carrying my unspoken fury like a bundle of firewood on my back. Still, when he would seek me out again, several days later, he would call me his "little scribe" and I — who had sworn to myself never to speak with him again — would converse and be proud of his attention.

"The lizard is in the crack and you, a giant, are outside waiting: think of its fear," he said, and sat down beside me. Taking a small bit of fallen plaster he poked it into the crack.

"Maybe it has a secret exit and is laughing at us," I said.

Eleazar shook his head. "A message has come from Jerusalem. The Romans have taken five thousand more men to send as slaves to Egypt — " I thought of the slaves I had seen in the port of Caesarea and wondered how many were alive and what might have happened to the one to whom I had given my ring — "They will take the young and leave me the women and the toothless ones!" I knew that Eleazar had been hoping for an uprising in Jerusalem. "Soon they shall spread us and we shall be like grains of sand in foreign soil. The fig trees of Judea shall shelter strangers."

I could say nothing for I knew that the spirit of the people was broken, and that no rebellion against the

Romans would take place before the babes who now suckled their mothers had hands strong enough to hold swords.

"But as long as we are here," he said, "as long as the Masada has not fallen, Judea still exists." Without realizing it I must have nodded, for Eleazar raised his voice. "Don't nod your head . . . David ben Joseph is your name but you are a little Greek; and you would go to Rome and be proud if they called you a citizen!"

His anger was unjust; and yet I must have felt there was the shadow of a truth in what he said, for I replied humbly, "I am here, not in Rome nor in Tyre."

A sarcastic smile disfigured Eleazar's face, "And why are you here?"

I looked down. The lizard had pushed aside the plaster and stuck out its head. "I don't know," I said, and to my dismay tears were forming in my eyes.

"You and my cousin Rachel will die here with us, but we shall die for Judea and you shall not know why you die."

I lifted my head, not caring whether he saw my tears. "You shall die for the desert and I will die for the pools of Ein-Gedi. I will die for the cool water and you — who hate Herod — will die for Herod's dream. We shall all die: such is God's Law — the rider and his horse and the shepherd and his flock . . . The lamb always twists its head when it is offered, to see the sky for the last time; and this I, too, shall do."

Eleazar's face was dark with anger but he was trying to control it. "You and Rachel are strong when you condemn others. What do you know of my loneliness, of my doubt?"

"It was not I who was judging, I was being judged."

Eleazar rose and shrugged his shoulders; and then I asked what I would not have dared to ask before, "Why will you not let Rachel go and take the children with her?" The anger returned to Eleazar's face, but I continued, "One child was sent away a month ago."

Eleazar walked to the edge of the pavement and looked out over the mountains. "That child was sick. It was a different matter. A war is not only fought between soldiers, it is fought between nations; and nations contain women and children." Suddenly Eleazar ben Ya'ir turned and looked with fury at me. "Do you think that I do not see the children when I walk by them? Do you think that I do not hear their laughter? I am a father, too. Three of the children on the Masada are mine. My youngest was born here. I gave him the name Jacob . . . Jacob, the father of the Children of Israel . . . Do you think that when I look upon him the thought does not occur to me that he shall be the father of no one? If I let doubt shine in my eyes and fear speak from my lips, would anyone but a fool follow me?" I bit my lip and Eleazar smiled. "A fool like you might, little scribe, but your arrows are only dangerous to those whom you do not aim them at, and no one on the Masada would dare to lend you a sling for fear of being responsible for someone being hit in the head with a stone."

I laughed, for it was true that I would never become a soldier; and though I was ashamed of it, I was pleased that Eleazar had noticed my miserable attempts without despising me.

"Rachel is my cousin by blood, so is her brother. I cannot let her or the children go, any more than I could send my own away."

"I know," I admitted. "I have tried to convince her with the same argument, but she does not understand."

Eleazar bent down beside me and looked at the column. "Where is the lizard?"

"I don't know," I said. "I haven't been watching."

"She always was that way, even when she was a child. She could not understand that even in games there were rules. It used to make me very angry." But Eleazar's face was not angry. Slowly he got up and walked towards the stairs. But before he ascended them, he turned, "When you are part of history, David, you are not allowed to be moved by a woman's tears. That too is a rule."

When he was gone, I sat and thought of Eleazar and of the history of Our People. Finally, I remembered the words of King David:

"*We have heard with our ears, Oh God, our fathers have told us, what work You did in their days, in the times of old.*"

The next verses I could not recall, but the end of the Song I knew well, for Simon ben Judas had repeated it over and over during the first days after the attempt to burn down his house:

"*Yea, for Your sake are we killed all the day long; we are counted as sheep for the slaughter.*

"*Awake, why do You sleep, Oh Lord? Arise, cast us not off forever.*

"*Why do You hide Your face, and forget our affliction and our oppression?*

"*For our soul is bowed down to the dust: our belly clings to the earth.*

"*Arise for our help, and redeem us for Your mercies' sake.*"

WINTER PASSED and summer came. The strong winds from the south blew. The memory of the few days of spring, when even on the Masada flowers grew, was gone. From all over Judea came bad tidings. Peace even at the price of slavery was the only ware sold in the marketplace. Our spirit might also have been broken, if it had not been for the Masada itself. We borrowed strength from the proud arrogance of King Herod. We read of the Maccabees and multiplied our numbers by dreams until we were as mighty as Rome.

A victory which cost us more than twenty dead was

hailed as if we had routed the whole Roman Army. And it may well have been that victory over a small force of Romans near the village of Tekoa that sealed our doom, for with it disappeared the possibility that the Romans would forget us. Among the dead was Rachel's brother; and now the two children had neither father nor mother. I had expected Rachel to beg Eleazar to let her leave with the orphaned children, but she did not.

We worked hard during the summer, trying to augment our supplies. The upper cisterns were filled with water and fuel was brought from Ein-Gedi. The most serious problem was our need of enough weapons to defend ourselves. We had few swords; but worse than that was our lack of arrows. Trees from the trunks of which shafts for arrows could be made did not grow in the wilderness; and as for metal arrowheads, we had very few. We placed rocks on the walls near all the gates, to be hurled on any attackers. Yet we still looked down the steep sides of the Masada and told ourselves that we were invincible.

"*By our Lord, who led us out of slavery, I beg of you . . .*" Eleazar ben Ya'ir paused and I looked up at him. I was writing a message to be sent to Jerusalem. "I won't beg. Write instead: *I command you to deliver unto these men as many weapons as can be found among the righteous men in Jerusalem. We are in dire need of arrows and arrowheads of metal. The silver the messengers bring may be used to purchase weapons from those who will not give them freely. The Lord has tempered our hearts and the enemy cannot break them.*" Eleazar looked at me angrily. It was a warning not to remind him what had been the answer to our previous messages to Jerusalem, to Joppa, to Bethlehem: That there were no weapons for the Romans had taken them away. "If every arrow on the Masada hit a Roman heart, we should still need ten times the number we have. And the best bowman will waste many an arrow."

The piece of parchment was small. There was hardly place for Eleazar to write his name. He had an awkward hand and it was difficult for him to make such small letters. "By the seven wells of Beersheba, I shall hold the Masada: This I swear! If God wishes that this mountain be stone for the offering of our flesh, then let it be so."

Eleazar had to stoop to go out through the opening of my room. The mat I used as a door fell back into place, and a line from one of the Songs of David came to my mind: "*Deliver me, Oh Lord, from the evil man: preserve me from the man of violence.*"

"David," Rachel whispered, lifted the mat and quickly entered my room.

"What is it?" I wanted to say that I was busy, but I have never been able to lie about such things.

"What did *he* want?"

"Nothing." It was because he feared that the palace where he kept his headquarters had too many ears that Eleazar came to my tiny room. "He sometimes comes here to talk with me," I said evasively.

"Do you know that Abraham from Dan deserted last night?"

I nodded but I said nothing.

"What will you do?"

I smiled. "I shall do nothing, but Eleazar has sent out a searching party . . . If it had been up to me, I would have sent a warning to the people of Dan that Abraham, the son of a donkey that was brought with Our People out of Egypt, will soon be among them braying again . . . But I hope Eleazar's party does not catch him. Eleazar has sworn to have him thrown over the wall at the steepest point of the Masada." Five men had already been executed in this manner, for crimes of murder and rebellion. I had seen it and had no wish to see it again.

"You know that you are no longer a boy." Rachel's voice was serious, but I chose not to notice it.

"My bar mitzvah is so long in the past that I have forgotten the expensive presents my father gave me."

"You have learned to say what you do not mean, and that is the sign of a man."

I looked away while I thought of something else to say.

"In Jerusalem, in the house of Simon ben Judas, you never spoke in the manner that you do now."

I could not explain to Rachel, when I did not know myself, what had happened to me. I used to look for her in order to talk with her, but now I avoided her.

"I asked Eleazar to send you away," she said.

"I know. He offered to let me leave, but I am staying."

Rachel smiled sadly. "Why, David? It is not for you to die here."

"That is for me to decide . . . now that I am a man."

Rachel walked to the doorway and lifted the mat. I almost called her back, to tell her that it was because I wanted to live so badly that I had decided to stay; but I didn't because I imagined myself saying the words and they seemed foolish.

It was at the end of the summer that our fate was determined. One afternoon it came marching: five thousand men, the advance guard of General Silva's army. We watched it from the walls. The sun glittered in the armor of the officers.

We felt relieved. We joked with each other and laughed, for when our escape was being cut off, our common destiny made us brothers. Only the sight of the children would bring a frown to the faces of the fathers. And men who were not used to showing affection would take their sons and daughters in their arms.

THE MASADA was surrounded. The wilderness below us was no longer an empty world of stones and sand. General Silva's army numbered more than ten thousand soldiers. The eagle's nest was under siege; and we were not eagles, for we could not fly away.

"Wait till the summer comes, then they will broil like chickens on a spit." Jesse took a stone and let it tumble down the side of the Masada.

"They won't wait for summer," I replied. I watched the stone bounce, hit a rock, and disappear from sight, long before it reached the bottom of the mountain.

"So much the better," Jesse said. He came from Jericho and was known as a fearless soldier. "They have built a wall around the Masada, for fear that we should attack them."

I looked at the man unbelievingly: had he really not understood the purpose of that wall, which the Romans had constructed around the base of the Masada? "It was not built to protect them. It is a net to catch us."

He shook his head and laughed. "Most of them are not even Greek. I could take on twenty without trouble."

I smiled for I knew he was brave: brave because he did not know fear, not because he had overcome it.

Rachel was coming out of the building near the palace where most of the important leaders lived. I turned my head quickly, in the hope that she would not recognize me.

"David," she called.

With a wave of my hand, I left my companion.

The sun was in her face and she squinted as she came towards me. "David, I looked for you yesterday. But you were not in your room or in your quarters."

"I was in the warehouses helping to measure out the weekly rations." I did not tell her that later I had been in the lower palace. I did not want to tell her of the place where I went to dream and to think.

"I want to talk with you." Her voice sounded desperate. "I can't talk now, but tonight . . . Meet me near the large cistern in the beginning of the second watch." She smiled nervously and for the first time I saw fear in her face.

By the end of the first of the watches of the night, most people on the Masada were asleep. Our guards at night were not numerous, for we did not fear an attack at night; whereas the Romans had a double night watch for it was during the night that our chance of escape was best. It was a dark night, the moon was but a sliver of silver in the sky.

So much had I not wanted to see Rachel that I had thought of not coming at all. She must have suspected this for she greeted me with relief, "I'm glad you have come," she said.

I didn't reply, for the night hid that I was blushing.

"Eleazar wants me to marry Joab!"

"No!" I exclaimed.

"Joab has one wife, but she is childless, and Eleazar says that Joab will take care of my brother's children."

Joab was a self-righteous man. He was the only one of our leaders who was hated. He was cruel, as well as brave. I did not like him, nor he me. "But why does Eleazar want this?"

Silently Rachel was crying. "He wants to destroy me. But we shall die, all of us. The Romans will kill us. Why must I die twice to please him?"

"Have you told him that you will not marry Joab?" I asked, although I knew that Eleazar as the nearest of kin to Rachel could force her to marry Joab.

"I did, and afterwards I could have bitten my tongue

into a thousand pieces and spit them in his face, for my refusal made him even more determined. If I had only said that I was pleased, he might have put off the marriage."

"But if we are all to die, does it matter?"

And Rachel answered with despair, "Oh David, you are such a child: You understand so much and yet so little."

The sorrow in her voice made me promise, "I shall speak to him."

"Tell him that I shall throw myself from the wall on the day of the marriage."

"No," I said angrily, "I shall not tell him that. One of the Commandments is: Thou shall not kill, and this forbids self-slaughter, as well . . . Job cursed his birth, but he did not kill himself . . . Man's life is God's gift. It is our glory, for if our few years break our spirit, how far are we from God, whose life is eternal?"

Rachel stamped her foot and almost shouted at me, "I curse the day that I learned to read. I curse words that are as the nets which fishermen use to catch the unsuspecting fish. Words that can make a young man into a self-important old man with a shaking finger. Tell Eleazar that I shall throw myself from the wall. And tell him that he shall not hear me scream while I fall."

"Rachel!" I called; but she walked away and did not turn around.

The voices of the guards shouting to each other filled the night and made my soul admit its loneliness.

After the morning prayers, I sought Eleazar. While I waited to speak with him, I tried to arrange my thoughts into the most convincing phrases, so that I could keep my promise to Rachel. But when I stood before him, all the words were gone, and I could think of nothing to say but, "Rachel will not marry Joab."

Eleazar's face grew dark, "And why will she not marry him?"

To my astonishment, I realized that I did not know why Rachel would not marry Joab. As unlucky as my first statement had been, so fortunate was my silence now. Eleazar's anger left him and he smiled, "Do you want to marry Rachel?" he said teasingly.

"She is my older . . . much older . . ." I stammered.

Eleazar laughed. "It would be a good marriage. Your father is wealthy; and it would benefit her relatives."

I did not like being laughed at, even by Eleazar, but I knew that it was wise to endure it. "I would marry her," I said.

Eleazar shook his head. "No, David, you are too young."

I felt my face flushing and I repeated my words, "I will marry her!"

"There is a knowledge that comes from age, and it is

well that youth does not possess it. Tell Rachel that I shall consider the problem again; but do not encourage her to be too hopeful, for there is no man on the Masada that I would rather give her to than Joab."

When I found Rachel and gave her Eleazar's message, she was pleased. "Did you tell him that I would jump from the wall?"

"No," I answered. "I didn't. I said that I would marry you myself."

Rachel looked at me strangely, but she did not laugh, and for this I was grateful.

THE SACRIFICE | 28

A NEW PLAN of the enemy made us forget our private worlds. The Roman army had brought with them about a hundred Jewish prisoners, who had labored building the camps of the soldiers. One afternoon there arrived several thousand prisoners. Some believed that they had been brought to be put to death in small groups before our eyes, to make us surrender the Masada; but soon we saw that it was in an another manner that they were to bring about our destruction.

At one point on the western side of the Masada, the distance to the bottom of the valley was not as profound as it was everywhere else; yet it was both steep and deep enough that none of us could have dreamt of General Silva's plan. He intended to build a ramp of stones and earth high enough to connect the walls of the Masada with one of the lower hills! On top he would build a road wide enough to bring up the tower with its battering ram. At first when we looked down the sides of the Masada and watched the tiny figures toiling, we thought it was a madman's idea. But four thousand men can carry many rocks and many baskets full of sand when they work from sunrise to sunset, and the music of the whip is on their back.

"They work them on the Sabbath!" The name of the man speaking was Isaac. He belonged to that little group of Essenes who lived among us.

"The Sabbath means nothing to them, but the coming of the summer wind does," I replied.

"Oh, they know," Isaac said sadly. "It is to insult us that they make them work, to insult us and our God."

Until now only the base of the ramp had been made, for it had to be very broad. "Will they be able to finish it before the summer comes?" an old man who had joined us asked.

I shrugged my shoulders. My companions wanted me to say no. This was a question we asked each other every day and to which was wanted only one answer. But I had begun to be convinced that the ramp could be finished before the worst heat came, so I no longer replied. I had seen the walls of Jerusalem and the Temple, and they had been demolished. I knew, too, that the Romans did not need to depend only on the prisoners for labor, they could use at least half of the soldiers as well. Auxiliary troops comprised more than half of General Silva's army and they could be ordered to do such work. The tenth legion would be held superior to the task, but they commanded the engines and the siege machines.

Isaac walked away. He could not bear to see people working on the Sabbath, breaking God's law to bring death upon us. He was a strongly built man with square shoulders. As I watched him walk away I thought, 'We people of the Law, Children of Israel, live close to our God, for we have only one God and his name is Jealousy. He has given us our life, chosen us; but he also demands of us that we live in Him. But the sect of Essenes are closer to Him, for they have chosen to live only in His shadow.'

A group of men, among them Eleazar and Joab, had come out of the small palace that they used as headquarters. Today Eleazar was not wearing his silver breastplate, but at his side hung his sword. Before the coming of the Romans, none but guards would wear weapons on the Sabbath. A child ran by and Eleazar bent down and took the child in his arms. I could not make out whether it was one of his own; but I knew that the face of the child would be serious and a little frightened. Eleazar tried often to play with his children, but he could not: Eleazar ben Ya'ir stood in the way of Eleazar the father. I thought of Eleazar's wife. She was a beautiful woman; but she seldom spoke and none of us knew her. She stayed in Eleazar's quarters and never came to the cistern to fetch water, there to gossip with the other women. An old woman, who probably was a relative of theirs, did the work. Though old in years, she was a child in mind. 'How strange that household must be,' I thought. I recalled my father's house in Tyre, my father whose heart was so easily moved that he never saw the smile in the beggar's eyes when he dropped a coin in his hand. Our house had been filled with laughter. Now I suddenly longed for it, longed to be a boy, awakening in my room and listening to the noises of the household.

When the evening prayers had been said and the sun had disappeared behind the mountains in the west and night was waiting to come, I grew restless. I walked the length of the Masada. I stopped to speak with those who were on guard at the upper level of Herod's northern palace. As it was impossible for anyone to climb the wall here at night, there were no guards at the lower levels.

The light had almost disappeared on the horizon when I reached the lowest terrace. Already the campfires of the Romans shone as the eyes of a beast in the night.

"Herod," I whispered, "what would you have done?"

From far away at the Roman camp, I could hear laughter. What were they laughing about?

My soul is weary of my life, I will leave my complaint upon myself, I will speak in the bitterness of my soul. These were Job's words . . . *I will speak in the bitterness of my soul.* How deep an impression they had made on me when I read the story of Job in the house of Simon ben Judas in Jerusalem . . . Should one ever speak from the bitterness? Should one not always gather what sweetness there lay in one's soul and speak from that? Multiplying the kindness given to me, the love shown, and from that sweet falseness make a world? . . . Now the stars shone mightily: the first watch had begun.

The falling of a stone tore me from my dreams. Someone was descending. I got up and hid myself behind a column. I knew who was coming, who was seeking the palace for the same reason I had: to be alone. The night was so still that I thought I could hear him breathing. I peeped out from behind the column and saw Eleazar ben Ya'ir. I was about to let him know I was there when I heard his voice; he was praying.

"Oh Lord, who led us out of Egypt, who guided the sword of David, and who in the time of the Maccabees brought glory to Judea, why do You forsake us now? Why have You taken David's sword from us and left us only Saul's? The bitter bread we shall eat and drink of the salt water. And yet we shall praise Your name, for while we eat of the bitter bread we may dream of the sweet. And while we drink the salt water we can remember the clear pools. Oh Lord, if we must perish, then let us die before our dreams! Take not from us the substance of our souls before our enemies still our bodies. Let us not be like those who are so old, that their minds cannot remember their youth, so that while we walk among the living, we are like the dead. If we must die, let us die praising life. Take from us our doubts. Turn not Your face from Your people to let them perish in a starless night."

I shook with fear for the naked soul of a man in pain is a fearful thing. From my eyes came tears. "Eleazar," I whispered, "Eleazar ben Ya'ir, it is I, the little scribe."

Eleazar laughed softly but without merriment. "I cannot escape you, little scribe. In my weakness you will be there to comfort me and in my strength to mock me. I wanted to talk with God and He sent me a stripling whose hand is better fitted for the writing reed than for the sword."

The half moon had come into the sky. "I had come here . . ." And then because the words that I had wanted to say had seem too great, I whispered, "To talk with myself."

Again Eleazar laughed, but this time his laughter was kinder.

I heard a strange cry almost like the whimper of a child, I looked down. At Eleazar's feet lay a young kid, its legs bound. It was one of twins born but a week ago to one of the few remaining goats on the Masada. Without being told, I knew Eleazar's purpose in bringing the animal.

"But only in the Temple in Jerusalem can offerings be made," I said.

Eleazar looked at the ground. "In ancient times, Our People made sacrifices in the land and any stone could be consecrated."

"But this is Herod's palace!" I exclaimed. I pointed to a seat near us. "That stone Herod commanded to be cut into a shape that pleased him. And some slave or workman did it."

"But the stone, was it not the land's? Was it not here when God was closer to us and we were but simple shepherds?" There was no shame in Eleazar's voice. "The Masada is His work, not Herod's. For Herod the towers and the walls, but for God the mountain!"

The spell of the night was upon us and the secrecy of the darkness inside us.

"You will help me afterward to make the burnt offering."

I looked up at the moon before I answered. The sky had been clear all day, but now, I saw a small cloud drawing near it. "I will," I agreed, though I knew we had no right to make the sacrifice.

Just as Eleazar placed his hand on the head of the kid, a cloud passed in front of the moon and cast the palace in shadow. I thought, 'Is that God in that cloud?

And what omen is there in the darkness?'

The cloud passed and again the light of the moon fell upon us. In front of one of the columns, we sprinkled the blood and made the burnt offering of the fat and kidneys.

"Leave me. I want to stay here a while." Eleazar's voice was so weary, as if he were asleep.

'Sorrow is his pillow,' I thought and I started towards the stairs. But before I left him, I turned and pleaded, "Don't make Rachel marry Joab. What little of life there is left to each of us must be our own."

Eleazar did not answer, and I climbed the broken stairs to the middle terrace.

Now I must hasten for I come to the fall of the Masada, the end of the war that the Jews fought against the might of Rome. But I do not believe, as some do, that this is the end of the Children of Israel. For as surely as we cannot break the Covenant that God made with us and must remain — even in our misery —His People, so He will not break the Covenant and destroy us.

The ramp grew and we could but watch it, having no power to interfere with its construction. My guess had been correct: Half of General Silva's army was now engaged in the work, the soldiers laboring side by side with the Jewish prisoners. Finally, the ramp was judged high enough and it was paved with stones into an almost perfect road. Now the machinery of the tenth legion could be brought up before Herod's wall to batter and destroy it.

The wooden tower, which General Silva had brought from Jerusalem, was rolled to within such a short distance of the Masada that the battering ram could pound the wall. I will not tell you of the battles we fought, since they were useless. Twice we made attempts during the night to attack the tower.

Our fate was sealed. Only God could save us and He chose not to. But in the acceptance of God's will, man still can make choices. Die we all must, but we need not die alike. Driven we were to slaughter, but need we die like beasts? God had cast us into misfortune; but He had not degraded us, for this man can only do unto himself.

Although all hope was gone, still we fought. When we realized that Herod's wall would give way, we constructed a new one. We reminded ourselves that we must not read God's Will in the actions of other men or the whims of nature, and be tempted to let the Sword of Justice fall from our hands or close our lips instead of speaking the truth. The Romans read their destiny in the entrails of birds, we read ours in the Torah and in Our Law. Our God has spoken to us; their gods are mute and therefore they must listen to the whispers in the wind.

The new wall was very cleverly constructed. We built it during a single night. We took beams from the larger of Herod's palaces and placed them in two rows, lengthwise and parallel, behind the breach that the battering ram was making. The space between the lines of beams, we filled with small pieces of wood and earth. This wall was soft and yet strong, for it absorbed the crushing weight of the battering ram. Each time the battering ram hit it, it became not weaker but stronger, as the force of the blows joined earth and wood together.

Yet even Herod's beams, made from the cedars of the Lebanon, carved with vines and clusters of grapes, could not save us.

"Eleazar wants you."

I was carrying stones to be used as missiles against the enemy. Eleazar had not spoken to me since the night of the offering. I placed the heavy stones on the pile and followed the messenger. He led me to the little palace that Eleazar used as his headquarters. Entering the first room, I recalled how I had waited there once before to speak with Eleazar; then he had been a hero clad in my dreams and I had been a boy following them.

"David . . ." Eleazar's face was stern but not with anger; and there was no sorrow in it, either. It was a mask; and had I seen more Greek plays then than in fact I had, I would have recognized it as the Mask of

Tragedy. For in tragedy man plays the role that the God has ordained and he is beyond unhappiness and beyond terror.

"We have lost, and even the smallest hope is not left to us. The trees have been cut from which our crosses are to be made; the chains of slavery forged that our women and children shall wear. I have a plan that shall rob the Romans of the fruit, at that very moment when their hands are stretching out to pluck it."

I looked away from Eleazar's face, for it frightened me.

"We shall kill ourselves, our women and our children, but first we shall set fire to what can burn and destroy what can be destroyed."

The words: "*You must take care of your life*," came to me and I spoke them aloud.

"Not your *life*, David, but your *soul.* God gave us life. It was a gift, but He owns only our soul. Should we choose for our women and children slavery, then we demean what does not belong to us."

" 'Thou shalt not kill,' so it is written," I said.

"Saul threw himself on his sword," Eleazar answered.

Then it was that I realized that although I had spoken of our death and had thought that there would be a last battle that we would lose, I had not really believed that we would die until now, when Eleazar talked of us killing ourselves. A wish to live as strong as the flow of rainwater, that makes riverbeds in the desert, flooded my mind. Yet I could not protest, for surely it was true that after our defeat all those still alive would either be crucified or sold into slavery.

"Each child who now plays on the Masada is worth so much silver. Each woman so much work or so much pleasure to our enemies. Why should we give them the triumph of finding them alive. Why should we pay them for our destruction?"

"Why not die fighting? Why not die with our swords in our hands?"

With his eyes closed, Eleazar answered me, as if I had not spoken those words but his own soul had whispered them. "The cries of our women, the tears of our children will lame our arms. Fear will lead us, once each man is alone surrounded by twenty of the enemy. Now we dream that we will fight, but when the swords against us are like the thorns of the thistle, then our will and our courage will falter."

Against my will, my thoughts whispered, 'I will not take my own life. I will be put to death or endure a life in slavery.'

Suddenly Eleazar's voice was soft, "Little scribe, you do not want to die?"

"No!" I confessed before I knew that I had spoken. "No, I do not want to die!"

Eleazar smiled and looked at me with strange tenderness. "You will not die. For just as it is our duty to die, it is yours to live and tell of our death. Who would have heard of Samson's courage and of his despair, had not someone told the tale and someone written it down.

You know that traitor Joseph ben Matthias. You will tell the Commander of Jotapata how Eleazar ben Ya'ir, Commander of the Masada, defended his fortress and how he died!"

"But if they crucify me, I shall not be able to write it down!"

The strange smile was still on Eleazar's lips. "They will not crucify you. Our death will guard your life. They will cart you off to Caesarea to tell the tale — to Rome, itself! It will tickle the emperor's ear; and for a moment, he will dream that he is Eleazar ben Ya'ir. In our defeat we shall be victorious; in all the world, our names shall be known. The destroyed Masada will stand again when children yet unborn will talk of us. We shall be like the dead leaves that fall upon the ground to make tomorrow's world green. Our deaths shall gain the freedom for Judea that our lives could not obtain."

I bowed my head. My mind was drinking Eleazar's words like wine, and I was drunk on words. The sight of my sandaled feet steadied me; and I did not dare look up.

"I have had this plan ever since the first Roman soldiers, like tiny insects, far below us, were sighted. But long I hoped that it would never be carried out . . . Each man will kill his own family and kin; then we shall offer our throats to each other, until only one man is alive; and he shall take his sword and end his life as Saul did."

"But if they will not kill their wives and children?"

Eleazar did not answer right away. When he did, his voice was low. "Then we shall die like slaughtered animals and the Romans shall be our butchers. And the Masada will be a mountain near the Sea of Salt, and nothing more."

I thought of Rachel: Would she allow anyone to kill her? Suddenly I understood why Eleazar had wanted her to marry Joab. If she remained unmarried, Eleazar was her nearest of kin. Hesitantly, I muttered, "Rachel . . . Rachel may not be willing — "

"She shall live, too . . . and the two children . . . I could not kill her against her will, though one day she may regret that she did not die with us . . . I have thought of a hiding place for you." Eleazar grinned, "So I shall give her her life." He turned his face from me. "With you there shall be two other children, who have no parents or kin on the Masada. It would not be right for us to kill them. Also, the old woman who tends my wife shall live. She is not capable of knowing the difference between life and death. Her mind has long ago gone. God took it from her. It would be unseeming for me to take her life. She is not even of Our People, but comes from Samaria."

I heard shouting outside. Eleazar's hand went to his sword. We both listened.

"There will be time for me to speak with you again, and tell you what Eleazar ben Ya'ir wants you to say to the world."

Again we heard shouts from the wall. "You will speak to no one of my plan. I will tell Rachel." Eleazar opened the door and hurried out of the palace.

I was alone. 'Is it wrong?' I thought. I remembered the cloud that had passed over the moon when we offered the goat kid. 'This is Herod's castle. Are these not Herod's dreams, born of pride? . . . The eagle and its nest, the horse and his rider?'

Again there was shouting from the wall. I walked out into midday sunlight which has no shadow.

THE FALL OF THE MASADA | 30

THEY ARE pulling the tower back!" the man next to me shouted triumphantly. "They can't crush the wall."

"No," I answered, and wondered to myself what new form of attack General Silva was contemplating. I walked to a place that was out of arrow shot and there climbed the wall.

The soldiers were pulling the tower back, moving its enormous weight on wooden rollers. It was much easier to move it backwards than it had been to move it up, for the ramp was built on an incline. Two officers were directing the operation. I heard them shouting and understood every word of their commands. When the tower had been brought back twenty paces, they halted. Bowmen took their stand again on the top platform. The tower was wooden but clad in iron, giving much protection to those inside it. From slits in the walls, they could shoot arrows, without running much risk of being hit themselves. In the lowest part of the tower on huge iron chains hung the battering ram.

The soldiers operating one of the catapults, which was placed far down the ramp, began hurling stones at us. I watched them fly in an arc over the wall.

I went to my old room. It was long since I had worked there. The ink in the inkwell was dry. From a jar, I poured a little water in the inkwell and stirred it with a stick. I dipped my reed and wrote on the back of my hand the word *hope*. I had tried myself to cure some skins in order to make parchment, but I had not succeeded. They hung in a corner of the room reminding me of my failure.

I thought of Eleazar's plan: Would I be able to write the story? Would I with words be able to construct the Masada? Would my breath be able to blow life into the still bodies of the defenders?

"Oh Lord," I prayed, "let me die, too!"

But already my mind was forming words from the pain of my knowledge. I wanted to scream out to God, 'Why didn't You create me as You did Eleazar?' But I did not for I knew his answer.

"David . . ."

I turned to look at Rachel. She was standing in the doorway, still holding the mat, so that the sharp light of the sun fell on her.

"Yes," I answered, wondering whether Eleazar had told her of his plan.

Rachel let the mat fall and stepped into the room. "David, your father is rich?"

I did not answer.

"When will the Greeks take the Masada?"

I shrugged my shoulders. "Tomorrow. Today. During the Passover Feast . . . How should I know?"

"But it will be soon?"

"Yes, it will be soon."

"What will happen to us? Will they kill us?"

I looked down at my reeds and the inkwell. "They will kill most of the men; the women and the children will be sold as slaves." But while I spoke I thought, 'So Eleazar has not told her yet.'

"Could you not write a message to your father? Tell him that he should buy me. I would serve him as a bondswoman not seven, but seven times seven years until I die, if he will buy the children and let them be brought up as free."

I laughed at the absurdity of the notion that I could now send a message from the Masada to Tyre.

"Your father will be in Jerusalem," she continued in spite of my laughter. "You are his first born. And I shall find means to get the message to him."

Abruptly, I stopped laughing and thought of what Rachel was saying. She was right! Any prisoners would probably be taken first to Jerusalem. And my father would come there, hoping to hear of me. And in my mind, I saw him standing before the crosses and seeing me, as I had seen the boy, Saul. I turned to Rachel angrily, "Why should my father save your brother's children? Why not someone else's? Why not Eleazar ben Ya'ir's?"

Avoiding my glance, Rachel muttered, "I don't know, David. I don't know."

"I know the children. Your niece and nephew are no better nor worse than any of the other children on the Masada!"

"You will not help me?" she whispered.

"I will!" I shouted and started to look for something to write on. And while I searched I spoke, and my words were like the lashing of a whip. "My father's heart is soft. I am his only son. Surely after my body is rotting on a cross or lies crushed in a ravine below the Masada, your nephew can usurp my place. He will be rich and his aunt's bonds will be light to wear, when clothed in linen. Then, surely, you will be able to say that the might of Rome is a blessing, since it gave you more than it took away!"

Having found a piece of skin on which I could write, I looked at her; she was pale and trembling. "I shall write that you were my friend and this Simon ben Judas can testify to. My father will cry and each tear will bind him to you and the children. I shall not write that I left Jerusalem because I wanted to search for you; for then, he would hate you for causing my death. I shall not write that I loved you but that you did not love me, but only thought to save yourself and your children by using my dead body, or he might think you odious."

"It is not true," Rachel sobbed and hid her face in her hands. "It is not true. You have grown to be a man, and your love is cruel and hard as most other men's. You lie, you did not come to search for me."

Instead of answering I laughed loudly and Rachel fled from my laughter, leaving me alone.

Later I did write a message to my father. I asked him to protect Rachel and the children and to buy their freedom. 'But I am not going to die,' I said to myself, 'and then I shall buy their freedom.'

But doubt came. The thought of being crucified filled me with terror. When Eleazar had said that they would not kill me, I had felt certain that he spoke the truth, that somehow he knew. But now I realized that he had spoken thus because I was a necessary part of his plan, of his dream.

"If I die, is it not just?" I whispered. "Have I not disobeyed my parents? Have I not broken the Law?" Then I thought, 'It is good I have written, for should I die through the pains of the cross, the pain would be worse if I had not written.'

When I stepped out of my room to look for Rachel

in order to give her the parchment, a terrifying sight met me. Beyond the new wall, smoke and flames were rising. The Romans had set fire to the beams and were trying to burn down the wall.

THERE WAS NOTHING we could do to prevent the burning of the wall. Our attempts to put out the fire, first with water and later with earth, were futile. It had become a raging fire almost at once. The cedars of the Lebanon had been dried by the winds of the desert for almost a hundred years. Only a change of wind could save us. For this we prayed: prayed to Our Lord, the God who had saved Our People in the past. For a moment when the fire was at its height we thought that He had heard, for the wind changed and blew the breath of the fire away from the wall, down the ramp towards the tower.

We shouted for joy! But it was not Our God who had heard us, only a whim of the wind, a jest of nature. Soon the wind blew again from the west and the fire ate the wall as a vulture the dead sheep. Night fell and the wind died down, but the wall was gone. The embers shined as the eyes of wolves.

We looked at each other and no one spoke. Each of us knew that the rising sun would be the signal for the attack. Through the breach in the wall, they would come by the thousands, and before the heat of midday the Masada would be theirs.

When I saw that the fire would not, by any means within our power, be extinguished, I looked for Eleazar ben Ya'ir. I found him walking with Joab and I did not approach him. Eleazar saw me but gave no notice of it until Joab left his side to fulfill some order that he had given him; then Eleazar beckoned to me. "I thought, little scribe, that I would have more time, but then it is not our custom to wait unduly with our funerals; and it would not be honorable to prolong this one because it is our own."

"Where is Rachel?" I asked.

"I have told her; and life was so warm in her veins that for a moment, I would have liked to still it."

Uncomfortably, I looked away.

"You would not understand, little scribe."

Swallowing my spittle, I murmured, "That is why you wanted to marry her to Joab, so he could do what you could not."

Eleazar laughed. "No, David, you have understood a little but not all. It is true that I have sometimes wanted to kill Rachel and I have never wanted to kill my wife. And yet I shall take the breath from my wife and that will be honorable, but if I killed Rachel it would be murder." Again Eleazar laughed; and his laughter was free, as if he knew no sorrow. "As soon as it gets dark, you are to meet Rachel by the great cistern. Below the wall, there is a cave. You are to take them there and then come back to me . . . You are my witness and my tongue, and the memory of us all."

Although I tried not to, I said, "But what if the Romans will not hear me? What if they kill me?"

Eleazar was not looking at me and for a moment I thought that he might not have heard me. "They will not kill you. God has meant for us to die, but he has not meant that our voices should be muted for all eternity. They will not kill you." Eleazar was calm, and his tone certain. "Go now, I have little time and much to do."

I turned and started to walk away; but Eleazar called, "Tell them that you are but thirteen. Your beardless chin will speak well for you."

Angrily I stopped and turned; but when I saw Eleazar ben Ya'ir's back, I felt a deep sense of shame.

When the sky in the west was almost dark, I went to the cistern. In the shadow of a small building which was used as a shed for goats, I met Rachel, the old woman who had been a servant to the wife of Eleazar, and the four children. The southern part of the Masada was unguarded, for those men who were not commanded to stand watch by the breach in the wall were to attend a meeting which Eleazar had called. Most of the women had taken their children and followed the men, not wanting to be alone in their despair.

A group of Essenes had once lived in the caves below the casement wall. The climb down was not difficult but the old woman complained because she did not understand why she must go with us. Only when I threatened to go to Eleazar and tell him that she would not obey me did she follow us.

Rachel had brought bread and water. Once we were in the cave, she fed the children and they grew quiet. I was eager to return to Eleazar. Rachel and I had hardly spoken, but when she saw me starting towards the entrance of the cave, she said, "Tell him that I would give my life for him . . . But not the children's. Tell him that . . ." I waited but Rachel said no more and I left.

By the smaller palace the men were gathered. A fire burned, throwing its flickering light on their faces. Behind the circles of men stood the women and children. Everyone was there; for so certain was Eleazar that the Romans would not attack during the night that now all guards had been withdrawn.

"My loyal followers, long ago we resolved to serve

neither the Romans nor anyone else but God, who alone is the true and righteous Lord of men." Eleazar ben Ya'ir was standing near the fire, so that everyone could see him. "We must not choose slavery now and with it penalties that will mean the end of everything, if we fall into the hands of the Romans. For we were the first to take up the struggle and shall be the last to break off the struggle . . ."

I looked at the men around me. Their faces were serious, they were listening; but what would happen when Eleazar told them of his plan? To kill themselves when it only meant robbing the Romans of their revenge — that they could be convinced of; but to persuade them to kill those they loved, could even Eleazar do this?

"Let us then pay the penalty, not to our enemies the Romans, but to God — by our own hands. It will be easier to bear. Let our wives die unabused, our children without the knowledge of slavery: after that, let us do each other an ungrudging kindness, preserving our freedom as a glorious winding sheet. But first let our possessions and the whole fortress go up in flames: It will be a bitter blow to the Romans, that I know, to find our persons beyond their reach and nothing left for them to loot. One thing only let us spare — our store of food: It will bear witness, when we are dead, to the fact that we perished, not through want, but because, as we resolved in the beginning, we chose death rather than slavery."

As Eleazar stopped speaking, I heard murmurs of assent, but also words of despair and defeat. His words had kindled a fire; but as yet the flames were so weak that a gust of wind could blow them out. In Eleazar's face there was a shadow of contempt and anger. Before anyone else could speak and with doubts destroy his plan, Eleazar shouted:

"I made a sad mistake in thinking that I had loyal supporters in the struggle for freedom, men resolved to live honorably or to die. You are no different from the common mob in courage or boldness, you who fear death even when it means the end of utter misery . . ." And Eleazar spoke of death: how like it was to sleep; and of the soul and of eternity. Some words he shouted like commands and some he whispered. And the words he shouted filled our heads and the words he whispered our hearts, until we were not ourselves, but all of us Eleazar ben Ya'ir.

He told of how our brothers were being killed like sheep. In Damascus eighteen thousand, in Egypt five thousand; and how in Caesarea on the Sabbath the streets had been rivers of Jewish blood. He talked of slavery and made us feel the fetters that we would wear, and gave us back for a moment the glory of war, now when it was lost.

"Let us die unenslaved by our enemies, and leave the world as free men in company with our wives and children. That is what the Law ordains, that is what our wives and children demand of us, the necessity God has laid on us, the opposite of what the Romans wish. They are anxious that none of us should die before the fortress is captured. So let us deny the enemy their hoped-for pleasure at our expense, and without more words leave them to be dumfounded by our death and awed by our courage."

A great shout came from the people, as if they had only one throat — and to my surprise, I was shouting, too.

I will not describe what happened for such a slaughter is unnatural to man: to kill not your enemy but those whom you love. Some of the children who died were so young that their breath was stopped before they had learned to speak . . . Why do I write this down — to bring a tear in the eye of a Roman Patrician? . . . No, let it be unguarded like stone: EACH MAN KILLED HIS OWN FAMILY. Let that sentence stand alone.

And now for the story of myself, for I did not die, I did not share my comrades' fate. When I shouted at the end of Eleazar's speech, I had resolved to die, and my hand grasped my knife. But at that moment, I saw Eleazar ben Ya'ir's glance resting upon me. Through the crowd I rushed up to him, to beg him for my death. But when I stood before him, I said nothing.

"Do you remember my words?" he asked and his eyes gleamed as burning embers.

"Yes," I whispered, although at that moment, I was not sure that I could remember.

"Many defeats have we suffered in this war, not only by the hand of the Romans, but also by our own. The defeat of the Masada must be our victory, this God has ordained. We are the last sacrifice, out of our death shall Judea again be free." He turned and I saw his wife and children were near him. I felt sick and weak as if I were going to faint.

Stumbling, I made my way through the crowd until I was alone. "I must live," I said aloud. Near me a shadow moved and I shivered with fear.

I ALMOST fell climbing down to the cave. When I stood at the opening, I heard the crying of a child. The moon was up and the valley below me was half in shadow and half in light. Inside the cave, it was dark. I called out Rachel's name, but she did not answer. When my eyes became accustomed to the darkness, I could see the children sitting with the old woman. The one who was crying she held on her lap.

"Where is Rachel?" I asked. The old woman did not answer. She was muttering a prayer to herself, moving her body back and forth.

I was about to go out and search for Rachel when

I heard stones fall. I knew she was coming. I was angry, furiously angry. "Where have you been?" I asked though I knew the answer to that question.

"I had to see him once more," she said and though her voice was filled with grief, it did not still my rage.

"Was it him, or was it his wife and children you went to see?" Rachel covered her face with her hands. "Go now," I shouted. "Go and see them now that they are dead and we are living. Go and praise your good heart, your kind soul. Tell Eleazar, if he is still alive, that you are braver than he!"

The children were crying. Rachel took her hands away from her face. In the moonlight I saw the features not of a living being, but the pale, still face of someone dead. "You are living, too," she said as she walked by me; and the tone of her voice was not angry nor sad, but lifeless.

I left the cave and climbed again to the top of the wall. My hands were shaking, and my legs were weak as if I had just overcome an almost fatal illness. I wanted to go to Eleazar to beg him to kill me, not to leave me alone. The sky was red. All the buildings on the northern part of the Masada were burning.

He would not do it, he would send me back. My hand touched the shaft of my knife. 'You are not a child,' I thought, 'who needs to beg adults to decide your life.' I drew the knife out of its sheath, and all the while I knew that I could not kill myself.

"You must take care of your soul," I whispered. And

then I smiled and thought, 'How often will you repeat those words and let God bear the guilt?' Then I answered myself, 'Until you are so old that memory will part from you and let peace come to your soul!' I stuck the knife back in my belt and sat down to watch the burning palaces.

Long I sat on the wall, until the moon was near setting and the fires began to die. When I knew that everyone was dead, although I was alone, I said prayers for their souls. But before I had done this, I had thrown my knife over the side of the Masada. Far away I heard the Romans call the watch. Soon the sky in the east would grow light with the coming sun.

When I entered the cave I called out Rachel's name softly. The children and the old woman were sleeping. She came to me and I whispered, "I am alive, too."

She took my hand but a moment later she let it drop. "We shall never know, shall we?" I asked.

"No, David, we shall never know," she answered.

I looked out over the ravine and the mountains beyond. It was growing lighter. "Death," I started to say, but said no more, for I would never know if death was easier than life. I had chosen to live and so had Rachel.

Until the morning when the light of the sun streamed over the mountains in the east, Rachel and I sat at the entrance of the cave. We did not speak to each other nor did we touch each other. Each sat alone and stared into the bleak landscape of the wilderness.

I heard the victorious shouts of the Roman army as the soldiers entered the fortress. I tried to close my mind to them. I looked at Rachel. Our eyes met but we did not speak. We rose and went to the children. I took the smallest one in my arms. For the last time we climbed the wall. The old woman whimpered as if she were a child. We walked along the top of the wall until the place where the steps led down to the Masada.

Smoke was coming from the buildings, the warehouses were still smoldering. The soldiers were there by the thousands. A group of them were pushing the others aside to make room for the officers to pass. Amongst them I recognized General Silva because of his gold breastplate. We walked towards them; we, the only survivors: four children; two women, one of them old and mad, and Rachel, who was the cousin of Eleazar ben Ya'ir; and I, David ben Joseph of Tyre.

Oh Herod, now your glory is gone! Men so low in station that you would not have talked with them will surpass you. The Masada will be Eleazar ben Ya'ir's, not yours. Men will seek this place not to see the ruins of your palaces, but in the dust of them to seek the footprint of Eleazar's sandaled feet. Children will hear of King Herod's madness: how he killed his own children; and they will shudder with repulsion, as when they first see a snake crawling through the dust. But when they hear of Eleazar their eyes will grow bright with longing; the blood he shed will be like a crown.

EPILOGUE

"You are free. You may go where you chose. Your father's money has come and has been duly paid. Also the woman and the two children who were with her are free. The cost to your father was great, I hope you will be grateful to him."

"I am grateful," I answered. I was in the villa of Joseph ben Matthias outside of Rome, where he is known as Flavius Josephus. Everything that Eleazar had prophesied had happened. I had even seen the emperor to tell him the story of the Masada.

"You are young. What shall you do? Be a merchant like your father?"

I shrugged my shoulders. "I do not know. I shall return to Tyre." There was no point in trying to explain to Joseph ben Matthias that I was no longer young. A child I had been and now I was a man; but the period in between, the time of youth, of dreams freed from reality, that period in life I would never experience.

"Do not brood over what happened to you, but learn from it. Serve the emperor; but serve him not so closely that when he falls, you need fall with him. The rider and his horse, that is the emperor — the kings — and God will always destroy them. Be near, but never be the stirrup that gains the king his seat in the saddle, for then God shall punish you as well."

I wanted to laugh because I had suddenly recalled our conversation, so long ago, in Caesarea, but I didn't. I thanked Joseph ben Matthias for his advice; and no doubt, he thought I had grown wiser.

"Eleazar wanted to be King of Judea. He did not know that there will be no more Jewish kings. The saddle had no stirrups and there was no horse. He was a fool. You have seen Rome and its vast glory. How could anyone coming out of the barren hills of Judea hope to tumble such a world?"

'Had he?' I asked myself silently, 'had Eleazar wanted to be king? Could he have conceived of Rome? . . . Yes, he had wanted to be king . . .' Aloud I said to Joseph ben Matthias, "Eleazar ben Ya'ir is dead. You have his last speech as Rachel and I wrote it down. You will include it in the history you are writing and men of future generations will read it."

Joseph ben Matthias smiled self-satisfiedly when I said his work would outlive his body. 'Vanity,' I thought and longed for the hills of Jerusalem, where the sky is nearer to the earth.

"I will include it. There were noble words in it. But as to his followers, they were only bandits, and do not expect me to write kindly of them."

Again I had to control myself in order not to smile; but to smile at Flavius Josephus to his face would be a dangerous affair. He had the ear of the emperor and did not care what lies he whispered into it.

"It is not bravery, young man, to be on the losing side, it is stupidity."

I nodded and thought, 'The day after tomorrow a ship leaves for Tyre. I shall sail on it and the fresh winds of the sea will blow. I shall visit my home and my mother shall cry when she sees me. And my father — he, too — will shed tears as a woman. I shall stay with them for a while and then — '

Joseph ben Matthias' voice interrupted my thoughts, "It is fine to be a merchant and fine to be rich, for wealth is a sign of God's approval."

I could not help shaking my head but Joseph ben Matthias did not notice. His words droned on and on as waves on the sea.

'To find God's meaning . . .' I thought. No, that